PUFFIN BOOKS

THE TWITS
NEXT DOOR

PUFFIN BOOKS

UK | USA | Canada | Ireland | Australia
India | New Zealand | South Africa

Penguin Books is part of the Penguin Random House group of companies
whose addresses can be found at global.penguinrandomhouse.com.

www.penguin.co.uk
www.puffin.co.uk
www.ladybird.co.uk

| Penguin
Random House
UK

First published 2024
001

Printed and bound in Great Britain by Clays Ltd, Elcograf S.p.A.

The authorized representative in the EEA is Penguin Random House Ireland,
Morrison Chambers, 32 Nassau Street, Dublin D02 YH68

A CIP catalogue record for this book is available from the British Library

HB ISBN: 978–0–241–698–34–1
TPB ISBN: 978–0–241–698–35–8

All correspondence to:
Puffin Books
Penguin Random House Children's
One Embassy Gardens, 8 Viaduct Gardens, London SW11 7BW

INSPIRED BY THE CHARACTERS OF

ROALD DAHL

THE TWITS NEXT DOOR

GREG JAMES & CHRIS SMITH

Illustrated by Emily Jones

PUFFIN

CONTENTS

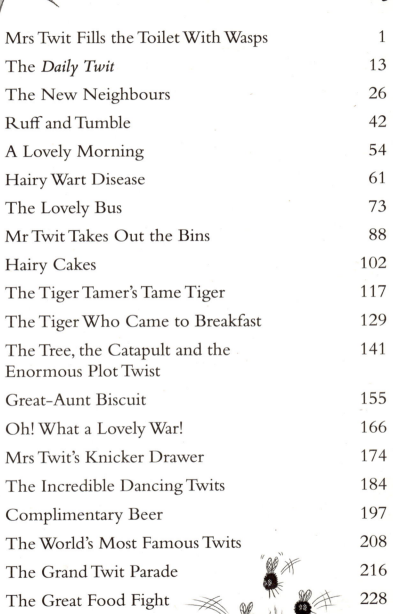

CHAPTER ONE

MRS TWIT FILLS THE TOILET WITH WASPS

Imagine what it must be like living next door to a pair of **TOTAL** **TWITS.**

What if you were unlucky enough to have **NOISY** twits as neighbours? The sort of people who play the trombone incredibly badly until four o'clock in the morning, or decide to start drilling into the walls while you're trying to have a lie-in?

Or imagine living next door to **NOSY** twits, who peer at you over the garden fence, or peep in through your windows while you're eating your tea.

What if some really **MESSY** twits moved in next door and filled their house with rubbish and their garden with rusty old cars?

Worse still, what if you lived next door to some **SMELLY** twits? Or some **MEAN** twits? Or some completely **HORRIBLE** twits, who are mean to your cat, or jump out at you from behind the garden fence dressed as clowns for no good reason?

All these are foul in their own way. But what if you were to end up living next door to a pair of twits who are

NOISY,
NOSY,
MESSY,
SMELLY,
MEAN and
HORRIBLE?

Do such appalling people really exist?

Well, sadly, yes they do. Their names are Mr and Mrs Twit and here they come now.

BRACE YOURSELVES.

Mr Twit has a face like a warthog's hairy armpit and a personality to match. There are many disgusting things about him, all the way from his dirty feet up to the hair on his head, which looks like the nest of the world's least house-proud bird. But the most disgusting thing about Mr Twit is his beard. It is as stiff and bristly as an old boot brush. And – even worse – it's full of the tiny morsels of food that miss Mr Twit's mouth as he eats his loathsome lunch or his sloppy supper. Clumps of **CURDLED** custard and puddles of **PUTRID** porridge nestle deep among the stubbly whiskers. And if he fancies a quick snack in between meals, Mr Twit simply sticks out his slimy tongue and sends it snaking through the beardy undergrowth in search of a tasty treat.

4

That's enough about that for now. It's too revolting to think about for more than a few seconds without getting a cramp in your brain. But there's more. You heard us mention **DIRTY FEET** a moment ago. Speaking of those, let's take a look at Mrs Twit.

Mrs Twit is a foul, screeching bundle of pure hideousness. She has a face like a scrunched-up elbow and her dress looks like a sack that fell on hard times sometime in the late eighteenth century. If you ever caught sight of her toenails, you would run home screaming for your mummy no matter how old you are. Mrs Twit's hobbies include shouting at kittens and knitting jumpers for puppies. She doesn't give the jumpers to the puppies, though – she makes the puppies

watch while she sets fire to them. That's the kind of thing Mrs Twit does for entertainment.

Mr and Mrs Twit live in a house that they built themselves, and as this story starts they do not have any next-door neighbours. That shouldn't come as a massive surprise. I mean, imagine living beside that pair. Or, indeed, beside that house. It is **DARK** and **DINGY,** because they built it without any windows to stop anyone from looking in at them. The garden is full of thistles and stinging nettles, and is surrounded by a high hedge of twisted brambles with sharp thorns to keep everybody out.

The reason for this is quite simple: Mr and Mrs Twit do not like other people. They don't even like each other. In fact, the list of things the Twits do not like is extremely long. It includes other people, being looked at by other people, talking to other people, other people living next door to them, each other, washing.

So what **DO** Mr and Mrs Twit like? That list is a lot shorter. And at the top of the list is this: playing

HORRIBLE, MEAN tricks on each other. And that is exactly where our story starts.

It was a fine fresh morning in springtime. The sun had just risen, casting a golden glow over the Big Dead Tree that sat in a clearing on one side of the Twits' garden. Mrs Twit was out and about bright and early that day, moving among the thistles with a large cloth-covered bucket clutched in one warty hand. She was wearing a tatty dressing gown and a wicked smile. This was because she was about to play a particularly painful prank on her horrible husband – one that she had been planning for several days. She was in such a good mood that she was even humming a merry little tune to herself. Although to most of us it wouldn't have sounded very merry or even much like a tune. It sounded like the screeching of rusty hinges.

'Where are you, my little lovelies?' croaked Mrs Twit, her knobbly back creaking as she bent down to hunt for something among the nettles. When she straightened up, she was holding a jam jar that was absolutely full of angry buzzing wasps.

The previous day, Mrs Twit had punched small holes into the lids of several jars and poured a small amount of honey into the bottom. This is how you make **WASP TRAPS** – the wasps crawl inside to get at the honey but can't find their way back through the holes. Carefully Mrs Twit unscrewed the lid of this first jar and tipped the wasps into her bucket, quickly putting the cloth back over the top. Then she moved on to her next trap. After half an hour, Mrs Twit's bucket was absolutely full to the brim with wasps. There must have been hundreds of them in there. Her smile grew wider and more wicked still.

Mrs Twit opened the front door of the house softly and crept inside. As you can imagine, the inside of the Twits' house was just as nasty as the outside. Everywhere you looked there was mess and neglect. The chairs were musty, the stairs were dusty, the oven was greasy and the toilet . . . well, we'll get to the toilet in a minute. But it's not going to be pretty.

Mrs Twit crept through the living room, across the kitchen and into the bathroom. And an apology is probably in order at this point. Because nobody wants to see inside Mr and Mrs Twit's bathroom, but it's part of the story, so we're just going to have to get through it somehow. As you can probably imagine, it's one of the worst rooms on the entire planet. For a start, as we already know, it doesn't have a window. Also, the bathroom has never been cleaned. Ever. Not once. **PLEASE ONLY LOOK AT THE FOLLOWING PICTURE IF YOU ATE OVER TWO HOURS AGO,** because it will probably make you feel sick, and these pages aren't as absorbent as they look.

READY?

THERE, TOLD YOU SO.
HORRIBLE, ISN'T IT?

But Mr and Mrs Twit didn't think it was horrible.
They hate things that are bright and clean, so this dark,
dank, dingy, dirty room was one of their favourites.
Every morning as soon as he got up,

Mr Twit would charge down the stairs straight to this bathroom and spend an hour sitting on the toilet and reading his newspaper.

'Hurry up in there, you smelly slop bucket!' Mrs Twit would shout, hammering on the door with the stick she always carried. (She didn't actually need a stick to walk; she just used it to thwack things.)

'Leave me alone!' the muffled voice of Mr Twit would reply from the other side of the locked door. 'I am reading my newspaper!'

'I NEED TO GO!' Mrs Twit would screech.

'I don't care!' Mr Twit would reply, smirking. 'You'll just have to cross your legs.'

This happened every morning for several years, and FINALLY an idea for revenge had come to Mrs Twit. Today she was putting her plan into action. Tiptoeing into the bathroom, she lifted the toilet seat and quickly upended the bucket on top of the toilet bowl. The wasps, who were growing tired of being cooped up, took this opportunity to make a bid for freedom and streamed down into the bowl.

Before they could realize their mistake, Mrs Twit had slammed the lid down on top of them with a bark of harsh laughter.

'This'll teach you to hog the toilet, you **MANGY DISHCLOTH!!'**

From upstairs a series of foul coughs and snorts told her that her husband had woken up. She heard the springs of the **SAGGY** old bed creaking as he levered himself to his feet, and then the clump of his footsteps heading towards the staircase.

Mrs Twit lowered herself into a greasy armchair in the living room and prepared to enjoy the fun.

CHAPTER TWO

THE *DAILY TWIT*

Mr Twit stomped down the stairs, his newspaper tucked under his arm. The newspaper was called the **DAILY TWIT** and it is not available in your local newsagent's. Mr Twit had made it himself and here is why.

Like many people, Mr Twit enjoyed catching up with the news each morning. But as he grew older, he realized that he only liked certain kinds of news. He really enjoyed reading about things that were sad, or things that were horrible, or things that were disgusting. And so Mr Twit began cutting these stories out of the newspaper and saving them in a special scrapbook that he called the **DAILY TWIT.** By now it was full of clippings about strange and unpleasant things. So each morning Mr Twit could amuse himself with headlines like

CAKE FACTORY CLOSES AFTER CUSTARD FLOOD

and

WORLD'S FLOOFIEST PUPPY ACCIDENTALLY SHAVED BALD IN CLIPPER ACCIDENT.

He particularly enjoyed one story from the local paper —

MAN DRIVES STEAMROLLER THROUGH PUMPKIN FESTIVAL

— because he had been the man in question.

Mr Twit reached the bottom of the stairs and peered suspiciously at Mrs Twit, who was sitting in her chair with a smug expression.

'What's wrong with your face?' he grunted.

'Whatever do you mean?' replied Mrs Twit.

'You look all . . . happy,' said Mr Twit, frowning. 'Cheerful,' he went on, scrunching up his face even further.

'No, no,' said Mrs Twit airily. 'I promise I'm not. You go and have a nice read of your newspaper.'

'Are you certain you're not PLOTTING something?' asked Mr Twit, now scowling so deeply that his hairy eyebrows tickled the end of his nose.

'Pinkie swear,' said Mrs Twit, holding up a little finger that looked like a mouldy chipolata.

'Hmm.' Mr Twit gave a final suspicious grunt and marched to the bathroom. Only then did Mrs Twit reveal her other hand, with two spongy sausage fingers firmly crossed.

In the bathroom, Mr Twit whipped his newspaper out from under his arm. Without looking behind him, he flipped up the toilet lid and plunked his twittish bottom down upon the seat.

Snickering, he began to read one of his favourite *Daily Twit* stories about a gang of criminals who had stolen all the presents from a hospital on Christmas Eve. Mr Twit chortled. **'PAHAHA!!'**

You're probably wondering by now what the wasps were up to.

WELL, LET'S FIND OUT, SHALL WE?

Yesterday they had been perfectly happy, just going about their waspy business. Wasps are really quite mild-mannered and calm if they're left alone. It's only when you bother them that things start to get sting-y. But these wasps had not been left alone – they had suddenly found themselves trapped inside jars. This had made them fairly **IRRITATED**. They had then been transferred to a crowded bucket.

At this point they had become seriously

ANNOYED.

When they had escaped the bucket, to find themselves in the world's worst toilet, they grew properly

ANGRY.

And this anger had turned into out-and-out

FURY

when Mr Twit's bottom had appeared from above, blotting out the sky like an incredibly unpleasant lunar eclipse.

Wasps spend a great deal of time being up close and personal with flowers, which are some of the nicest things in the world. Mr Twit's bottom is about as far away from a lovely flower as you can get – see the following table for reference:

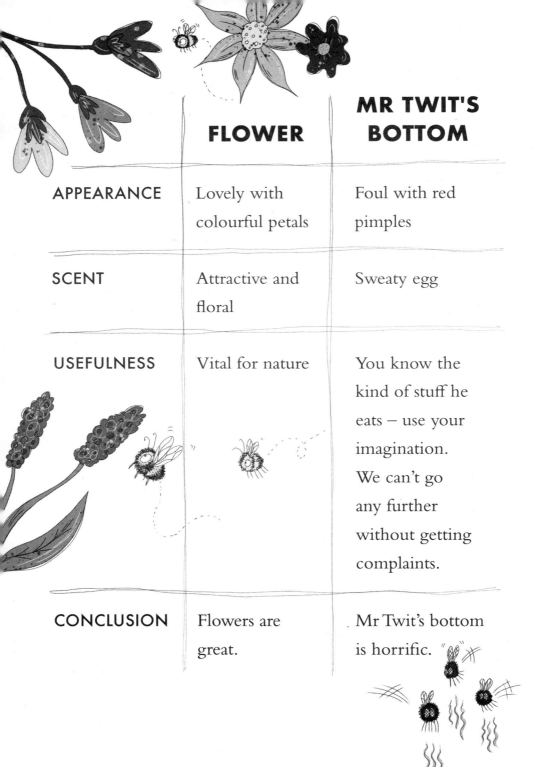

	FLOWER	**MR TWIT'S BOTTOM**
APPEARANCE	Lovely with colourful petals	Foul with red pimples
SCENT	Attractive and floral	Sweaty egg
USEFULNESS	Vital for nature	You know the kind of stuff he eats – use your imagination. We can't go any further without getting complaints.
CONCLUSION	Flowers are great.	Mr Twit's bottom is horrific.

With nothing to lose and the alternative being completely disgusting, the wasps decided they would have to mount an attack in a desperate bid for freedom. Stings at the ready, they surged upwards towards the incoming moon. And, as one, they plunged their barbs into its craggy cratered surface.

Midway through reading the news story, a change came over Mr Twit's face. His expression of mean glee was replaced by one of white-hot horror. His eyes widened so much that it looked as if they were about to

POP OUT
ON STALKS.

His face went so red that it looked as if it was about to

BURST INTO **FLAMES.**

A noise like a steam train in agony came

SPOUTING OUT OF HIS NOSE.

And he shot straight up from the toilet as if it was a volcano that had just erupted with burning lava. Indeed, that was exactly what it felt like as hundreds of wasps stung his bottom at the same time.

'GWAAARRRGGGHHHHH,'

roared Mr Twit, racing through the living room as best he could with his trousers round his ankles, his bare rear end covered with furious wasps like a moving carpet.

'Whatever is the matter, my dear?' said Mrs Twit, rising from her chair and carefully concealing her expression of wicked delight. 'Has something gone amiss in the toilet department?'

'MY **BOTTOM'S** ON **FIRE!**' roared Mr Twit, twisting and capering around like a firework that's escaped the box. The wasps took this opportunity to escape, streaming out underneath the front door and flying as far away from the Twits and their toilet as was waspishly possible.

'Oh, dearie me,' said Mrs Twit. 'Hold on a moment – I've got just the thing. Don't go anywhere!'

She reached beneath her chair and pulled out a gigantic round tub. A label on the side read

PEACHY FEELGOOD'S
SUPER-SOOTHING
BOTTOM BALM

'Sit yourself down in that,' she instructed, unscrewing the lid and shoving the tub towards her husband. 'You'll feel better in no time.'

Mr Twit, with a quick glance at the label, threw himself bottom first on top of the tub with a squeak of relief.

We **REWIND** at this point to the previous afternoon. After carefully setting her wasp traps around the garden, Mrs Twit had put on her coat and walked into town. She had stopped at two different shops – a chemist and a grocery store. At the chemist's she had bought their very largest tub of PEACHY FEELGOOD'S SUPER-SOOTHING BOTTOM BALM. And at the grocery store she had purchased an equally large tub marked

OL' STEAMY'S
XXXX EXTRA-HOT
DEATH-WISH
GHOST-CHILLI SAUCE

It was marked with several warning labels, including one saying **DO NOT ALLOW TO COME INTO CONTACT WITH SKIN** and a large picture of a skull with flames coming out of its mouth. Once home, Mrs Twit had carefully scooped the bottom balm into the kitchen bin and filled the tub to the brim with Ol' Steamy's.

When he sank his wasp-stung bottom into this tub, Mr Twit's brain was fully expecting to feel a lovely cool sensation of relief. It took several seconds for his nerves to register that this was not, in fact, what was happening. Instead his entire rear area was immersed in what felt like pure liquid pain. He gave a shriek like a factory whistle and ran straight out through the front door without bothering to open it. The door was so old and rickety that it simply splintered into pieces.

Mr Twit stampeded through the prickly under-growth like a runaway bin lorry. His panicked eyes caught sight of the garden pond, and he leaped into the air and dive-bombed into it bottom first, sending up a large hiss and a cloud of steam. Mrs Twit, who had followed him through the nettles, doubled over at the side of the pond, slapping her knobbly knees with pleasure and cackling at the top of her voice.

'That'll teach you to hog the toilet all morning, you sour-faced sauerkraut!' she yelled.

'My bottom's never going to be the same again!' roared Mr Twit, thrashing around in the greenish stagnant water. Several outraged frogs hopped away carrying small suitcases, having suddenly decided to emigrate.

It was only after several minutes that Mr and Mrs Twit became aware that something strange was going on. Something that had not happened for many years.

Mr Twit **STOPPED THRASHING**.

Mrs Twit **STOPPED CACKLING**.

They both slowly turned to look towards the edge of their garden.

Two rather unusual people were looking over a low section of the hedge, staring at the Twits with matching expressions of wide-eyed horror.

CHAPTER THREE

THE NEW NEIGHBOURS

If you have good thoughts, as somebody wise once said, they will shine out of your face like sunbeams and you will always look lovely.

But what happens if you have mean thoughts? Nothing but mean, angry thoughts – day after day, year after year, decade after decade?

THE ANSWER IS HORRIFYING.
PUT DOWN THAT BISCUIT AND STEEL YOURSELF.

If you think nothing but mean thoughts, then after a while the mean thoughts will start to breed inside your heart like a nest of wriggling **EARWIGS**. Every mean thought will shrivel up your face a tiny bit more until it **SQUASHES** backwards into a permanent scowl. Mean thoughts drag the corners of your mouth downwards until you look grumpy and cross all the time.

You see, mean thoughts turn you inwards. Nice people are always looking around, seeing how they can make other people's days better. They face outwards and are curious about the world around them and the people who live in it. But mean people are entirely turned inwards, jealously guarding their wicked thoughts like a dragon guards its treasure. That was what had happened to Mr and Mrs Twit.

But what about the people who were staring at them over the prickly hedge?

Mr and Mrs Lovely had nothing but good thoughts all day and every day. Because of this, their faces were open and shining with happiness. Here, as we meet them for the first time, they were looking a little less happy than usual because they were watching a horrible man thrashing around in a stagnant pond and yelling about how much his bottom hurt. **IT'S ENOUGH TO TAKE THE SHINE OFF ANYONE'S DAY**, even if you're as completely and utterly lovely as Mr and Mrs Lovely.

Mrs Lovely quickly pulled herself together. Replacing her look of horror with a cheery smile, she waved at Mrs Twit over the hedge and called out a friendly **'HELLO!'**

'What do you mean?' replied Mrs Twit, scowling. People never said 'hello' to Mrs Twit. They said things like,

'STOP SHOUTING AT MY KITTEN,'

or

'GET OUT OF MY GARDEN,'

or

'GIVE MY CHILD HIS ICE CREAM BACK.'

This reaction caught Mrs Lovely rather by surprise. 'Erm . . . hello?' she repeated uncertainly.

By now Mr Twit was sloshing his way out of the pond. He heaved himself upright and waddled to the edge, his sopping-wet trousers puddled round his ankles. And together Mr and Mrs Twit took a long hard look at the two strangers on the other side of their hedge.

Mr Lovely was dressed in a jaunty blazer in stripes of yellow and purple — his two favourite colours. He had a small neat beard that was as far away from Mr Twit's beard as you are from Earendel, the most distant star in the known universe **(TRUE FACT)**. On his head he wore the kind of round straw hat that is called a boater, with a purple ribbon tied round it. He was also wearing a happy smile and an extremely smart pair of trousers. Mr Twit hated and distrusted him on sight.

While Mr Twit was staring at Mr Lovely and feeling the beginnings of a deep and satisfying dislike, something even stranger was happening to Mrs Twit.

LET'S

PAUSE

AND TAKE

A CLOSE

LOOK

AT IT.

Remember the bit at the start of this chapter? You know – **NICE THOUGHTS, SHINE, FACE, SUNBEAMS?** All that stuff? Well, imagine for a moment there's a magic mirror that shows you what you might have looked like if your life had gone in a completely different direction. If you've been on the mean side, it would show you how lovely you'd look if you'd had nice thoughts instead. And the other way round too. That was exactly how Mrs Twit and Mrs Lovely felt as they gazed across the hedge at each other.

Like her husband, Mrs Lovely was dressed mainly in yellow and purple. She wore purple dungarees over a yellow T-shirt. On her feet she wore big black work boots.

Mrs Twit's scowl deepened. She had the strangest feeling that Mrs Lovely was familiar, but she simply could not work out how.

Anyway, we can't hang about watching people stare at each other over a hedge all day. It would make for a very boring chapter.

LET'S GET BACK TO THE STORY.
WHERE WERE WE? AH YES.

'Erm . . . hello?' repeated Mrs Lovely uncertainly.

'**HE-LLO?**' echoed Mrs Twit scornfully, as if she'd never heard the word before.

'**HELLO!**' bellowed Mr Lovely in reply, waving his stripe-clad arm enthusiastically. 'Hello, hello, hello to our new neighbours! I say, that looked like a lovely refreshing dip you were having! I love swimming too!'

He beamed at Mr Twit, who was now standing beside the pond with weed in his hair, tadpoles in his jacket pockets and – let's not forget – his trousers still round his ankles. His long shirt tails dripped dirty pondwater down his hairy legs.

'We're the Lovelies!' declared Mrs Lovely, her grin growing wider. 'We're really looking forward to getting to know you!'

Both the Twits stared at her as if she had just said,

'FAFFLE WOOF PTANG COMBINE HARVESTER MAM-MAM.'

Which she hadn't. That would have been silly.

'We're just moving in!' added Mr Lovely. 'Isn't that splendid?'

Once again, the Twits simply gaped at him as if he'd danced around the garden barking like a seal.

'We're your new next-door neighbours!' shouted Mrs Lovely, hoping that this would get the message across. But if she was hoping for a reply like 'Oh, new NEIGHBOURS! How charming! Do come straight round for a cup of tea and a plate of fresh cookies!' she was about to be disappointed. In fact, disappointment was an emotion that Mrs Lovely was going to become very friendly with indeed over the next few weeks.

With a horrified grunt, Mrs Twit turned and vanished into the thistles. Mr Twit, hopping awkwardly as he tried to pull his wet trousers back up, followed her as quickly as he could – which as you can imagine was not particularly quickly. Within a few seconds they had disappeared back towards their dark, windowless house.

Mr and Mrs Lovely turned to exchange a look of complete **BRAIN-BUFFETED BEMUSEMENT.**

Panting like two pairs of filthy old bellows, Mr and Mrs Twit threw themselves into their house.

'SAVE ME, MR TWIT!' wailed Mrs Twit, sinking down into her chair. 'My legs feel all **WOBBLY!** That was the worst moment of my entire life!'

'Did you see them?' said Mr Twit faintly, passing a hand over his sweating brow. 'Just standing there behind OUR hedge . . . **LOOKING AT US!'**

'And TALKING TO US!' squealed Mrs Twit. **'LOOKING AND TALKING RIGHT AT US!'**

As we discovered earlier, Mr and Mrs Twit hated other people, and they hated being looked at by them. It's true of most horrible people – and you can prove it with a simple experiment. Next time someone behaves in a foul way towards you, simply stand there and look at them. You don't need to say anything, just take a long hard look. They will very quickly become jumpy and uncomfortable. Horrible people can't stand being looked at closely. Perhaps, somewhere very deep inside, they are aware of how unpleasant they are and there are some stirrings of embarrassment. But, whatever the reason, they can't stand it.

Mr and Mrs Twit had gone to very great lengths to avoid being looked at: building their house without windows, filling the garden with spiky and stinging plants and so on. The thought of actually having next-door neighbours filled their entire bodies with an unbearable **WRIGGLING, SQUIRMY** feeling of discomfort.

'She said they're our neighbours!' said Mrs Twit, massaging her tummy to try to squash the uncomfortable feeling. 'Are they really moving into the empty house next door? I don't think I can stand it!'

Mr Twit scratched his beard thoughtfully, dislodging a piece of hard-boiled egg that had been dangling at the edge of his chin since January.

'I shall go and see what's happening,' he declared, feeling rather brave and wise. 'I shall climb up the tree with my telescope.'

'Oh yes, DO!' Mrs Twit felt quite desperate at the thought of OTHER PEOPLE so nearby. 'Go and see what they're up to!' She closed her eyes as a fresh wave of horror trickled down her body like a bucket of chilled sick.

Mr Twit marched to the cupboard, pulled out a rusty telescope and took it with him into the garden. Tucking the telescope under his arm, he carefully climbed the wooden ladder that was propped against the Big Dead Tree. Once at the top, he threw his leg over the widest branch and settled himself back against the trunk. In his horrible old suit he was almost invisible against the gnarled wood. The only things you could really see were **HIS EYES** surrounded by a thick tangle of hair and beard. It looked as if a bad-tempered owl was peering out of a hole, but otherwise he was perfectly camouflaged. Mr Twit lifted the telescope and peered next door. What he saw almost made him fall off his perch.

A bright red removal van was parked in the street and people were carrying boxes and crates up the garden path. The house itself, which had been empty for several years, had grown rather damp and rundown. But today the windows were open, and busy sounds of

HAMMERING,
HOOVERING AND
CLEANING were coming from inside.

As Mr Twit watched, Mrs Lovely came **SKIPPING** out of the front door wearing a large tub on her back like a rucksack. This was attached to a pipe with a nozzle on the end. Mrs Lovely flicked a switch and yellow paint began to shoot out of the nozzle.

Within a few minutes the front of the house was freshly painted.

'What a disgusting colour,' muttered Mr Twit to himself. 'Looks like phlegm.'

In fact, it didn't. It looked incredibly bright and cheerful. But Mr Twit didn't like bright, cheerful things.

Mr Twit stayed in the tree for several hours watching Mr and Mrs Lovely moving into their new house. By then the entire house was painted bright yellow, with purple curtains hanging at each window. Peering into these windows, he could see that the inside of the house had been swept and cleaned. Furniture in a selection of bright colours had been carried in by the removal workers, and Mr and Mrs Lovely were sitting down, sharing a pot of tea. The pot, in case you're wondering, was also bright yellow and the tea, **NATURALLY,** was lovely.

Mr Twit slid back down the ladder to report these terrifying developments to Mrs Twit. This meant

that he completely missed what happened next –
something that would have made him

MORE **HORRIFIED** STILL.

CHAPTER FOUR

RUFF AND TUMBLE

What happened next was this: a second removal van pulled up outside the Lovelies' new house, and two children jumped out of it and ran excitedly into the garden.

Now that probably doesn't sound particularly horrifying to you. But to Mr and Mrs Twit it would have been one of the worst possible things ever.

THEY HATED CHILDREN.

They hated the way children are **BRIGHT** and **CURIOUS** and **ENERGETIC**. They hated the way children stick up for each other. Mr and Mrs

Twit must have been children themselves once — there's no way round that, as far as we know — but, as with many twits before and since, they had stopped being children as soon as possible and immediately forgotten what it was like.

The two children were Mr and Mrs Lovely's twins. They were ten years old and their names were Ruff and Tumble. Well, actually, they weren't. They were called Raff and Taylor. But nobody had used those names since they were babies — everybody referred to them as Ruff and Tumble for reasons that are about to become clear.

'This garden is amazing!' shouted Ruff, doing a forward roll and disappearing into a thicket of brambles. 'It's like a jungle!'

Because the house next to Mr and Mrs Twit had been deserted for several years, the garden had run completely **WILD.** The grass had grown to head height and was full of tall thistles that had sprouted from seeds blown in from the Twits' garden. The many trees and bushes were overgrown and heavy with blossom, which made their branches bend right down to the ground to make interesting dens and tunnels. It was an absolutely perfect place to play – and playing outdoors was what Ruff and Tumble liked to do best.

'Just look at this place!' said Tumble, turning round on the spot to take in her new home.

Her twin brother was nowhere to be seen.

'Hey!' she shouted. 'Where did you go?'

There was a rustling sound from the thicket and she peered inside. A pine cone came whizzing out and hit her squarely on the nose.

'I'll get you for that!' she yelled, plunging into the undergrowth in hot pursuit.

Yes, Ruff and Tumble loved to play outdoors. Any kind of games, really: pirates, explorers, astronauts – basically anything that involved chasing each other and fighting. It wasn't that they didn't like each other – they were actually great friends – but they just loved play-fighting. It had been like this since they were toddlers, when their favourite game had been to put metal wastepaper baskets on their heads and race each other around the house, bumping into the walls and each other. Their clothes were always ripped and their faces smudgy. They loved

RUNNING,

JUMPING,

CHASING and

SCRAPPING.

They loved it even more than they loved mint choc-chip ice cream. And they loved that very much indeed.

Mr and Mrs Lovely were far too lovely to play these kinds of games with their children. Again and again, they would try to encourage them to settle down with a **NICE JIGSAW** or have a **NICE AFTERNOON BAKING A CAKE**. But the twins just ended up flinging jigsaw pieces at each other, and baking quickly descended into a food fight that covered the kitchen in flour and eggs. This is the reason that Ruff and Tumble had been kept out of the way for most of moving day; it would have been impossible to tidy or paint the house without the whole process turning into a very messy battlefield. But now they were here, ready to explore their new home. And because they loved to be outdoors more than anything, they were starting with the garden.

'Children!' fluted Mrs Lovely from the back doorstep. 'Are you going to come and have a look at your new bedrooms?'

There was a suspicious **RUSTLING** from the tall grasses nearby and a muffled **'OUCH!'**

'Not yet, Mum!' came Tumble's voice. 'We're still exploring the garden! It's brilliant out here!'

Mrs Lovely looked around at the wild wilderness. 'But it's terrible!' she said. 'It's so untidy!'

'That's why we love it!' replied Tumble, who was hiding with her brother.

'They're going to cut all this down and make the

garden super boring, aren't they?' said Ruff mournfully as Mrs Lovely went back inside. He was sitting beside his sister with his hair full of dandelion leaves.

Tumble nodded. 'Uh-huh. Before we know it, they'll make it all . . . you know, *lovely*. Flower beds and all that kind of nonsense.'

'Well, let's make the most of it for as long as we can,' Ruff told her. 'Last one up that big tree gets a dead leg!'

And, pausing only to give his sister a friendly push, he sprinted off towards an enormous horse chestnut tree that stood near the hedge, spreading its branches right across the Lovely family's new garden. One thick branch even stuck out right across the prickly hedge and into Twit territory.

When the twins reached the bottom of the tree and looked up, they both let out gasps of surprise and delight. There, in the branches above them, was the most incredible tree house they had ever seen. It was sturdily built of very old dark wood, cradled securely where the main trunk of the tree split off into three giant branches. The tree house had been put there many years ago, even before Mr and Mrs Twit had built their horrible windowless house next door. And there it had stayed, protected by the thick canopy of twigs and leaves overhead, waiting for new owners.

'**COME ON!**' yelled Tumble, reaching for a low branch and swinging herself upwards.

Both twins were excellent tree climbers but, to be honest, it didn't really matter. A series of short, stout branches stuck out from the trunk on the side nearest the hedge, forming a natural ladder. Within a minute or so they had both hauled themselves up on to the wooden platform. And, once there, they could truly appreciate how amazing the tree house really was.

Some tree houses are little more than a few planks nailed together. The slightly better ones might have a makeshift roof or even a couple of rickety walls. This one had a proper roof, which was watertight and sloping so the rain could run off. The walls were made of thick planks, and in each one was a proper glass window. The whole structure was firmly set on the platform, which was lashed to the branches with

coils of rope that looked like they might have come from a sailing ship. The door was low – deliberately too low for grown-ups to get inside comfortably. In short, it was the greatest tree house ever.

'I don't care what our new bedrooms are like,' said Tumble, her eyes wide. 'I am totally living here.'

'Yeah,' said Ruff. 'Mum and Dad can have the boring house that isn't in a tree.' Reaching out, he turned the door handle and the twins wriggled inside.

The tree house smelled of old wood and fresh air. Even though it had lain empty for years, it had been so well built that nothing had rotted or broken. It had been preserved like a time capsule. An oil lantern was standing in one corner beside a camping stove with a kettle on top, and a pair of binoculars dangled from a hook beside the window that looked over the garden. Tumble grabbed these and flicked the catch that opened the window. They had a clear view of the Twits' house, standing tall and dark in its thistle-filled garden, with the afternoon sunlight casting a spiky shadow of the Big Dead Tree over the windowless walls.

'**WHOA!**' breathed Tumble, gazing through the binoculars. 'I wonder who lives THERE! Just **LOOK** at that place!'

Ruff joined her at the window. 'Who builds a house like that?' he wondered out loud. The house next door gave him a strange **SHIVERY** feeling.

Tumble was moving the binoculars around, getting a good look at this odd rickety house. After a while she trained the lenses on the dead tree on one side of the garden. She frowned, and tried to focus more carefully. There was an odd darker-brown patch near the trunk and what looked like a twig-filled hole above it. Something glinted in the middle of it. It was, of course, Mr Twit peering back through his telescope. He was so startled to find somebody staring right back at him that he **TUMBLED OFF HIS BRANCH,**

falling into a patch of nettles with a **SQUAWK.**

51

Later, when the twins had finally been persuaded to climb down from the tree house for an important moving-in day ritual, the First Night Takeaway, Ruff asked, 'Mum? Who lives in that freaky old house next door?'

All four members of the Lovely family were gathered round the kitchen table tucking into delicious noodles and dumplings.

'Oh yes,' said Mrs Lovely. 'The next-door neighbours. Your father and I had a little chat with them earlier on. They seem . . .' Mrs Lovely searched her brain for the right word as the twins fought over the last prawn cracker. She was an extremely lovely person and never had a bad word to say about anyone. Unfortunately the only suitable words to describe Mr and Mrs Twit were all bad ones.

'They seem very **INTERESTING** people!' broke in Mr Lovely.

'Yes, that's right!' agreed Mrs Lovely. '**INTERESTING!** That's the exact word.'

It wasn't. The exact word is **UNPRINTABLE.**

'I'm sure that the more we get to know them, the more we'll like them,' she went on hopefully.

'Mmmm,' said Tumble doubtfully, catching her brother's eye.

Her parents had never met anybody they didn't get on with, but there was something about the house next door that made her suspect that was about to change. And she was

ABSOLUTELY

ONE HUNDRED PER CENT

CORRECT.

CHAPTER FIVE
A LOVELY MORNING

One week later, the house next door to Mr and Mrs Twit had been completely transformed. When Mr and Mrs Lovely had moved in, it had been rundown and neglected. But the Lovelies had worked hard day and night, and now it looked brand new. Remember when Mrs Twit first saw Mrs Lovely? And how it was as if a magic mirror was showing her what she might have looked like if she had had good thoughts all her life? Well, it now looked as if a giant magic mirror had been stretched between the two gardens. The Twits' house – dark, uncared-for and altogether un-pleasant-looking – now stood beside its exact opposite.

Mr and Mrs Lovely's house was spotless and painted bright yellow with purple window ledges and guttering. The garden surrounding it was beautifully neat and tidy, with a perfect stripy green lawn bordered by colourful beds of spring flowers. And inside, as you can imagine, things were just as **LOVELY**.

When Mrs Lovely came downstairs one morning, Mr Lovely was in the kitchen making chocolate pancakes for breakfast. The delicious smell filled the whole house.

How **LOVELY**, thought Mrs Lovely to herself, as she did every single morning of her **LOVELY** life.

'Good morning, my **LOVELY** wife,' said Mr Lovely, kissing her tenderly on the cheek. 'Would you like a cup of hot chocolate?' Many grown-ups have coffee in the morning, but that isn't sweet enough for the Lovelies.

'Oh yes, that would be **LOVELY**,' replied Mrs Lovely. 'But whatever is this?' Her eye had been caught by a large box in the middle of the dining table. It was neatly wrapped in purple paper, with a yellow bow on top.

'It's a **LOVELY** present for you, Mrs Lovely!' announced Mr Lovely, beaming. 'Isn't that **LOVELY?'**

'A present?' said Mrs Lovely excitedly. 'But it isn't my birthday, Mr Lovely!'

'No! But it's so **LOVELY** getting a present that I thought I'd buy you one anyway! It'll give you a **LOVELY** day today – just like the **LOVELY CODE** says!'

Mrs Lovely sat down at the table and began to untie the yellow ribbon.

On the wall of the living room was a large, framed piece of embroidery that said the following:

THE LOVELY CODE

Be lovely at all times to everybody
Give everybody a lovely day
Everybody is lovely underneath

These words were surrounded by delicate hand-stitched flowers, butterflies, cherubs, gambolling lambs and other similarly **LOVELY** things. The Lovely Code embodied the three rules that Mr and Mrs Lovely lived by every single day of their **LOVELY** lives.

Having untied the ribbon, Mrs Lovely neatly folded back the purple paper to reveal a box. She opened the lid to reveal a large cream-filled cake.

'Oh, Mr Lovely!' exclaimed Mrs Lovely. 'That cake looks absolutely —'

'**LOVELY?**' interrupted Mr Lovely. 'It does, doesn't it? Cake always makes the day more **LOVELY**, I find.'

Mrs Lovely clapped her hands in delight. 'How **LOVELY!**'

As you may have started to realize, Mr and Mrs Lovely could be a bit much if you spent a great deal of time in their company. Too much loveliness can become a little overwhelming. Ruff and Tumble certainly thought so — which is partly why they had been so pleased to discover the tree house, where they could relax without everything having to be quite so **LOVELY** all the time.

The enormous horse chestnut tree with the tree house half hidden among its bright new leaves was the only thing in the Lovely garden that hadn't been pruned, trimmed and tidied. True to their word, Ruff and Tumble had claimed the tree house to be their bedroom and on the very first night had carried mattresses and quilts up into the branches. There they had spent most of the week play-fighting while their parents beavered away below. They only came inside for meals – and now it was breakfast time.

'Morning, Mum! Morning, Dad!' said Tumble, racing hungrily into the kitchen, followed by her brother. 'What's for breakfast?'

'Lovely, lovely chocolate pancakes!' Mr Lovely told her.

'Oh, cool,' Tumble replied, grabbing one and cramming it into her mouth all at once.

'Don't eat your pancakes like that, dear,' complained Mr Lovely. 'It's not lovely!'

Tumble rolled her eyes as she spoke through a mouthful of half-chewed pancake: 'Dad, not everything and everybody has to be lovely all the time, you know!'

Both her parents gasped in shock.

'I've asked you before – PLEASE don't say that!' said Mrs Lovely, who had gone rather pale. 'Remember the Lovely Code! **EVERYBODY IS LOVELY UNDERNEATH!**' She pointed to the cross-stitched words on the wall.

'I'm not sure that's right, you know,' said Ruff, who was also eating a pancake with his fingers. 'Not EVERYBODY is lovely. What about that horrible couple next door?'

'You mean our INTERESTING neighbours?' said Mrs Lovely. 'I'm quite sure they're lovely underneath.'

At this point a decidedly unlovely noise floated in

through the kitchen window. From next door came
the sound of

SCREECHING,

RUNNING FEET,

A **DEEP** CROAKY VOICE

SHOUTING and a strange

COMMOTION.

All four Lovelies rushed outside to see what on
earth was going on.

CHAPTER SIX

HAIRY WART DISEASE

The twins hadn't been the only people who had spent a lot of the week concealed in a tree. Each morning Mr Twit had taken up his position in the Big Dead Tree to see what was going on next door. And with each passing day he had become more and more horrified as the Lovely house and garden grew **LOVELIER AND LOVELIER**. He had nearly been caught at one point when he had watched Mr Lovely going round the garden hugging each individual tree.

'FAUGH!' Mr Twit had spat out in disgust.

'What was that?' called Mr Lovely, pausing while tenderly embracing a silver birch. 'Is someone there?'

'KA-KAAAARK!'

Mr Twit had squawked in what he hoped was a good imitation of a bird. In fact, it sounded more like a pterodactyl stubbing its toe.

Mr Lovely had peered across into the Twits' garden, but he'd been unable to pick out Mr Twit in his brown clothes. He'd shrugged and gone back to his tree-hugging.

'Thank you for being *you*,' Mr Lovely had said to a nearby sapling, giving it a friendly stroke.

Mr Twit had made sure to keep his disgust to himself from that point onwards.

Apart from the flower beds, which he hated, and the neat lawn, which he also hated, two other things had appeared in the Lovely garden that week that Mr Twit found extremely distressing. The first was the large modern workshop that had been built near the hedge. It had windows that overlooked the garden and a thick metal chimney. Mr Twit had his own workshed, which was **RICKETY** and **FILTHY,** in which he invented mean tricks to make Mrs Twit's life miserable. The workshop next door, which belonged to Mrs Lovely, was for the opposite purpose and we shall find out all about it soon.

The second thing that had appeared that made Mr Twit's skin itch with irritation was the strange vehicle that was now parked in front of the Lovely family's house. It looked a bit like one of those food trucks that serve burgers at the roadside. It had a hatch that ran all along one side. In cheerful yellow and purple letters above this hatch were the words **'LOVELY THINGS'**. This was Mr and Mrs Lovely's pride and joy – and, once again, more details are coming very soon. But we've got something unpleasant to get out of the way first. Because up in his tree Mr Twit had been plotting.

Mr Twit already knew he was going to have to try to get rid of this dreadful new family. But he had some unfinished business to take care of first.

He needed to take revenge on Mrs Twit for her trick with the wasps. His bottom was still swollen and sore – it was covered in stings that had now started to go purple and bluish. If you'd been unlucky enough to catch a glimpse of him without his trousers on, you might have thought he was a cross-looking baboon.

One morning, a week or so after the Lovelies had moved in, Mr and Mrs Twit were fast asleep in their dank drab beds in their dark, damp house. Because their bedroom had no windows, like the rest of the house, the only light was a faint glow coming down the chimney into the cold fireplace. Both Twits were sleeping on their backs and letting out the most enormous snores you ever heard. It sounded like two giant woodpeckers hammering their beaks into squashy rotten wood.

Presently Mr Twit woke himself up with an unusually **LOUD SNORE.** He gave a **GURGLING** cough and opened one eye.

'Another day,' he muttered, peering over at the dim light on the hearth. 'Ah, well. No rest for the twittish. Better get on with it, I suppose.'

He rolled himself out of bed and collected a large metal bucket that he'd hidden behind his bedside table. He had spent the last week filling this bucket with caterpillars, choosing the fattest and hairiest ones that he could find crawling around on the nettles in the garden.

As softly as Santa (who the Twits hated, by the way – he never brought them anything), Mr Twit crept across the bedroom. He pulled back the bottom of Mrs Twit's blanket and carefully tipped the caterpillars in before tucking the blanket back in again. Then he lay down in his own bed and waited, chuckling quietly to himself.

After a few minutes, Mrs Twit's snores stopped. She mumbled to herself in her sleep as the caterpillars began to march across her bare feet and up her legs. When they reached her tummy, she suddenly sat bolt upright.

Mr Twit pretended he had just woken up. He marched across the bedroom and pulled back her blanket.

'You've got a **TERRIBLE CASE OF HAIRY WARTS,'** he said, pointing to one particularly large caterpillar, which was now making its way out of the top of her nightgown. 'Look! There's a big hairy one breaking out on your shoulder right now!'

Mrs Twit peered sideways and saw something large, green and hairy on her shoulder.

'WARRGH!'

she cried, leaping out of bed and hopping around the bedroom.

She looked down to see that her legs were completely coated with fuzzy moving lumps.

'IT'S THE HAIRY WARTS!' she wailed. 'You're right, Mr Twit! Oh, what's to become of me?'

'If you're not treated straight away,' said Mr Twit, hopping from foot to foot in excitement, 'then before long your whole body will become one giant hairy green wart. Then you'll grow bigger and bigger until . . . **POP!**

You'll burst like a ripe spot. And nothing will be left of you but green goo.'

'NOOOOO!'

cried Mrs Twit. 'I don't want to burst! I don't want to be goo!'

'You need to pop all the hairy warts without delay!' Mr Twit told her seriously. 'Before they spread. You must go into the garden and roll about in the thistles to pop as many as you can. And because I am kind and generous I shall bring you your thwacking stick so you can get any extra ones that you miss.'

'Quickly then!' Mrs Twit urged him. 'I think I can feel them spreading already!'

And with a quavering howl like a wild anteater, she galumphed down the stairs in her bare feet and threw open the front door, which had been fixed with rickety planks from the workshed. Not far away was an especially large patch of tall thick-stemmed thistles with huge spiky heads. Mrs Twit chucked herself into these like an Olympic diver and began rolling back and forth, screaming like a **BANSHEE.**

Mr Twit encouraged her from the doorway, where he was standing holding her stick. 'That's it! Pop those warts! Pop them all! Roll for all you're worth, you silly sandwich!'

'GWAAARRRGH!'

foghorned Mrs Twit as the sharp thistles pricked her leathery hide all over. (The caterpillars were all managing to escape into the undergrowth if you're worried.) 'Have I got them?' she asked, struggling to her feet with her nightgown in tatters. 'Am I unwarted?'

'Almost,' said Mr Twit, a nasty leer spreading across his mean face. 'I can see a few you've missed. But fear not! Here!' And he threw her stick. Mrs Twit caught it and began poking at herself all over, trying to dislodge the caterpillars that were still crawling about.

'MEARGH!' shouted Mrs Twit. 'It tickles!'

'Keep prodding!' he told her. 'The hairy warts are spreading already! It's almost too late!'

Which brings us back to the Lovely family having their chocolate pancakes in the kitchen. They rushed outside to find Mr Twit chortling as he watched his wife galloping around the garden poking at herself with her stick. The Lovelies gaped at them over the hedge. For the first time in their lives they were completely unable to find anything lovely to say.

'GO AWAY, WARTS!' bellowed Mrs Twit, cantering through a thistle patch with a few caterpillars clinging to her face and shoulders. As Mr and Mrs Lovely and Ruff and Tumble watched, she managed to flick one off her shoulder and it pinged off into the distance, uttering a tiny **WHEEEEEEE!'**

'Everybody's lovely underneath, eh?' said Tumble to her mother.

'Is everything quite all right, Mrs Twit?' called Mrs Lovely.

At this Mrs Twit stopped cantering and Mr Twit stopped chortling.

'It's those **OTHER PEOPLE** again,' said Mrs Twit.

Remember, the Twits hate other people.
'LOOKING AT US,' added Mr Twit.

'And there are **CHILDREN,'** gasped out Mrs Twit, feeling her skin going all itchy – and not just because of the caterpillars.

'Is there anything we can do to help?' offered Mr Lovely. He felt sure that whatever was going on was not in the least lovely. It was challenging his entire world view.

'I've got a bad case of hairy wart disease!' said Mrs Twit. 'We need to pop the warts before I turn into goo!' And she prepared to dive back into the thistles.

'**STOP!**' yelled Mr Lovely frantically. 'You'll hurt yourself!'

'THAT'S THE WHOLE IDEA!' barked Mr Twit angrily.

Mr Lovely was extremely shocked by this. 'That's not very lovely, is it?' he asked slightly weakly.

'**WHO WANTS TO BE LOVELY?**' said Mrs Twit.

'Well . . . everybody!' said Mrs Lovely. 'Everybody is lovely underneath! It says so on our living-room wall.'

'Well, we're not,' Mr Twit told her.

'I simply refuse to believe that,' said Mrs Lovely firmly. '**EVERYBODY IS LOVELY UNDERNEATH!**' she called over her shoulder as she marched down the garden towards her workshop. And Mrs Twit, satisfied that the Hairy Warts had been cured, staggered back inside for breakfast.

CHAPTER SEVEN

THE LOVELY BUS

We promised earlier that you would soon find out what happens inside the workshop in the Lovelies' garden.

AND THE TIME HAS NOW COME.

If you were paying attention, you may have noticed that at the end of the last chapter Mrs Lovely was walking towards this very building. You are probably now hopping about, going, 'Is it time to find out what happens in the workshop? Is it, is it, IS IT?' Well, calm down, please. **YOU MIGHT WET YOURSELF.** Yes, it is indeed time to find out all about it. And the finding-out process shall begin . . .

NOW.

Mrs Lovely can invent just about anything you want. She has a marvellous workshop full of wheels and wire and buckets of glue and balls of string and huge pots full of thick foaming stuff that gives off smoke in many colours. And in this workshop she spends her time coming up with incredible inventions.

What are these incredible things that Mrs Lovely works so hard at inventing? Well, it all has to do with the LOVELY CODE that hangs in her living room. Item two of this code reads:

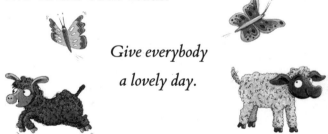

Give everybody
a lovely day.

And Mrs Lovely spends a great deal of her time coming up with marvellous concoctions and contraptions to try to make that happen. Here are some of the Lovely Things she has created:

TWINKLE BOMBS: instead of stink bombs, which smell horrible, Mrs Lovely invented Twinkle Bombs, which smell wonderful. You can throw them discreetly and treat someone to the scent of clean laundry or a meadow full of flowers or the seaside at sunrise. **LOVELY.**

WELLY WARMER: pour this very clever powder into someone's wellington boots, and when they put them on they will feel toasty warm.

INSTANT BALL PIT: everybody loves playing in a ball pit. (Well, as long as it's clean. Imagine a ball pit after Mr Twit's been rolling about in it. Yuck.) This incredible invention from Mrs Lovely will turn any room into a ball pit. It looks a bit like one giant ball, but when you throw it, hundreds of smaller ones pop out. **INSTANT PARTY!**

DISCO PANTS: dancing will cheer anyone up, but some people are too shy to start. For this reason Mrs Lovely invented Disco Pants. They look like a normal pair of pants (although they are bright purple with yellow trim), but when you put them on, you won't be able to resist having a little boogie. **GUARANTEED SMILES!**

SURPRISE CAKE: it looks like a tiny cake on wheels. But set it rolling towards somebody and, when it reaches them, it will miraculously transform into a full-sized cake. **ICING AMBUSH!**

POPCORN GRENADE: this bomb will release oodles of hot delicious popcorn when you toss it towards someone. Sweet or salted varieties are available. Or why not throw two at a time and enjoy a mixture?

Those are just a few of Mrs Lovely's many inventions – all of them designed to make your day a little bit more lovely. A few years ago, she had inherited a great deal of money from a relative and, together with her husband, had decided to travel the land spreading Lovely Things to as many people as possible. And to do this they used the vehicle we saw parked in front of their house – **THE LOVELY BUS**.

The Lovely Bus was powered by Mr Lovely, who sat in the driving seat at the front and pedalled it like a bicycle. Mrs Lovely sat in the back, surrounded by all the wonderful things she had invented in her workshop, with the twins as her helpers when they weren't at school. Together they set out to **GIVE EVERYBODY A LOVELY DAY.**

This particular day hadn't started out in a very lovely way, thanks to Mrs Twit and her hairy warts. But Mrs Lovely soon forgot all about them as she loaded up the Lovely Bus and prepared to put the Lovely Code into action once again.

Mr Lovely turned the handlebars to the left as he

pedalled away from their home. With a cheery **TING** on his bell, he steered the bus through the town centre and into the back streets. After a while, the Lovely Bus was trundling along a rather dingy-looking street.

'I say, Mrs Lovely,' called Mr Lovely over his shoulder, 'this part of town doesn't look particularly lovely, does it?'

Mrs Lovely stuck her head out of a small window behind the driver's seat.

'No, it certainly doesn't,' she said, looking around. 'Stop the bus, Mr Lovely! It's time to give some people a lovely day!'

Mr Lovely pulled a large lever next to him that operated the brakes and the Lovely Bus came to a halt by the kerb. Then Mrs Lovely opened the long hatch that ran along one side of the bus. Once this was held in place with a stout stick, she flicked a series of switches. There was whirring from hidden machinery and, after a few seconds, the Lovely Bus began its work.

From a chimney on the bus's roof a stream of

different-coloured **BUBBLES** began to float along the street. Multicoloured lights flashed on the sides of the bus, and cheerful music began to trickle out of several concealed speakers. Mrs Lovely stepped down from the bus wearing the same backpack and nozzle that Mr Twit had seen her using to paint the house. The twins followed, each wearing similar backpacks and grinning expectantly.

'Now follow my lead as usual, children,' said Mrs Lovely. 'Let's start over there!' She pointed to an old, drab-looking house near the end of the street. With Ruff and Tumble following, she walked towards it.

'This house isn't very lovely at all, is it?' she called back over her shoulder. 'Imagine living there! Those people must hardly ever have a lovely day! But we can soon change that.' She reached the house and pulled the trigger on her paint sprayer. A jet of bright yellow paint shot out of the nozzle, and within seconds the house was completely repainted.

'OI!' said a man from behind her. 'What do you think you're doing? That's my house!'

'You're welcome!' said Mrs Lovely in a sing-song voice. 'Don't worry – there's more to come! Ruff! Tumble! Your turn!'

This was the twins' favourite part of helping their parents give people a lovely day. Ruff aimed his own paint sprayer at the front of the newly yellow house and it gave a **POP-POP-POPPING**

sound as he pulled the trigger. He fired a series of red blobs, which landed on the front wall with a splat and immediately turned into small painted flowers.

'What on earth do you think you're doing?' asked the man again, staring up at his bright yellow and now flower-dotted wall.

'Isn't it lovely?' shouted Mrs Lovely.

'Not really, no –' the man started to say.

But before he could finish, Tumble had aimed her nozzle at his front door. Soon it was covered with messy splodges of purple paint.

'We're making your house more lovely for you!' explained Mr Lovely, approaching with a large bag in his hand. 'Would you like a Lovely Hat?'

'Eh?' said the man.

'A Lovely Hat!' said Mr Lovely, reaching in the bag and pulling out a purple hat shaped like his own straw boater. 'Everything's more lovely when you're wearing a hat! Here you go! **LOVELY!'** He plonked the hat on the startled man's head and marched back to the Lovely Bus. Mrs Lovely and the twins followed.

'But I don't want a hat,' protested the man weakly. 'And I don't even like purple. Or flowers.' But nobody was listening to him. The bubbles, lights and music had already drawn quite a crowd.

'Who wants **CUPCAKES?'** yelled Mr Lovely, and several people put up their hands and cheered. Mr Lovely jumped into the bus and grabbed something that looked like a large tube with a handle on the top. 'This is Mrs Lovely's latest invention!' he announced. 'It's the **CUPCAKE CANNON!** Get ready!'

By now the whole crowd was **FIZZING** with excitement. Mr Lovely pressed a button and cupcakes began to shoot out of the tube across the heads of the assembled people. They were iced in bright colours and people leaped to try to catch one. The twins, who had taken off their backpacks, joined in. They weren't going to pass up the chance of free cake. On the other side of the road, Mrs Lovely was now repainting another house in a shocking shade of pink.

Mr and Mrs Lovely and the twins spent several hours on the street, giving everyone who lived there a thoroughly lovely day. There was face-painting for the children and plenty of cake for everybody. At one point Mrs Lovely surprised the crowd with the Instant Ball Pit. She set up a large high-sided paddling pool in the street and threw a big bouncy ball into the centre. When it landed it popped, sending out hundreds of smaller balls that filled the pool. Ruff and Tumble were the first to dive in. And then finally, when everybody had finished playing in the Instant Ball Pit, it was time for the Lovelies' finale.

'We've enjoyed making your day lovely,' said Mrs Lovely, 'but it's almost time to go.'

'I still don't want a yellow house,' complained the man in the purple Lovely Hat, but again nobody paid attention to him. They were too excited to find out what lovely thing would happen next.

'Before we leave, though,' Mrs Lovely went on, 'here's something to finish off the day in the loveliest way! I like to call this invention – **DISCO PANTS!**

Who fancies a little dance?'

The crowd cheered.

'THREE . . .

TWO . . .

ONE . . .

PANTS!'

yelled Mrs Lovely, and she pushed a purple button inside the Lovely Bus.

With a boom, hundreds of pairs of Disco Pants were launched into the air from the roof of the bus. They fluttered down into the street like a multicoloured Y-fronted parachute display team. Ruff and Tumble were some of the first to grab pants and pull them on – these were their favourite Lovely invention. The crowd followed suit and soon everyone in the street was wearing a pair of bright purple pants.

Mr Lovely turned up the music and, as the Disco Pants activated, everybody began to dance around. Soon the whole street was laughing as they **JIGGED** about to the Lovelies' upbeat tunes.

'Have you had a good time?' Mr Lovely asked an older lady near the front. She had a walking frame but had still managed to pull on a pair of Disco Pants and was now doing a little **SHUFFLY** dance in her slippers.

'Ooh, yes!' she told him. 'I hadn't been out of the house in two weeks! And today I've had a cake, I've had my face painted and I'm having a dance for the first time in years!' She had her whole face painted like a flower, by the way. We probably should have mentioned that earlier. 'It's been **LOVELY!**' she told Mr Lovely.

'That's what we're here for!' he replied with a cheery wave. 'Come on then, Mrs Lovely,' he called. 'I think our work here is done!'

He leaped back into the driving seat. Mrs Lovely climbed in, the twins following, and closed the hatch.

Mr Lovely released the brake and began to pedal and, with a **TING** of the bell, the Lovely Bus rolled away, leaving a street full of happy dancing people. All apart from one man, who was still complaining that he'd preferred his house when it was the old colour. But nobody took him seriously because he was wearing a purple hat.

CHAPTER EIGHT

MR TWIT TAKES OUT THE BINS

A few mornings later, Mr Twit was at the side of his house where the Twits' two metal dustbins were kept. You know what the inside of the Twits' house is like, so you can picture what their bins were like. They were the **DIRTIEST, SMELLIEST, RUSTIEST** pair of bins you have ever seen – full to the brim with rotten food and filthy old rubbish. Think about the disgusting things that Mr and Mrs Twit like to eat: mouldy sardines, boiled tripe, cauliflower that has gone all brown and floppy, minced pickled eggs . . . We could go on, but we won't. Now imagine for a second what this pair of nasty twits might throw away.

What could be so foul that even they wouldn't eat it? That is the stuff that goes in their dustbins.

Grumbling to himself, Mr Twit removed the dustbin lids, dropping them to the ground with a

GIANT CLANG.

He picked up both bins by the handles on the side and hefted them over his shoulder. He picked his way through the tall nettles and thistles to a low point in the brambly hedge and tipped the bins over. An avalanche of foul-smelling filth landed – with a moist **SQUELCH** – in one of Mr Lovely's prized flower beds.

'There,' said Mr Twit, 'that's one of my chores done. Time for breakfast.'

He replaced the lids on the bins, again making as much noise as possible, and went back into the house.

Now obviously this is not the normal way to take out the bins. We just need to point that out in case you're ever asked to help — we don't want a pile of angry letters from your families. But Mr and Mrs Twit had made an important decision. They had decided that

THE LOVELY FAMILY
MUST GO.

Mr and Mrs Twit did not like other people. They had built their house without windows to avoid being looked at or spoken to. And now they had Mr and Mrs Lovely living next door — who were so lovely that it was simply **UNBEARABLE.** They were always popping up over the hedge, saying irritating things like 'Good morning' or 'Isn't it a lovely day?' or 'Do you need anything from the shops?' Whenever this happened, the Twits would scurry back inside without speaking. They couldn't stand the loveliness, you see.

'DAD!' shouted Tumble, coming in from the

garden. 'That **HORRIBLE HAIRY WOMBAT** from next door has just tipped his bins into your flower beds again!' (This was the third morning in a row that this had happened.)

Mr Lovely rushed to the back door. 'Oh dear,' he said. 'Not again! My lovely daffodils! I wonder if it was foxes.'

'How many times do I have to tell you?' said Tumble angrily. 'It was not FOXES. It was TWITS! They're being horrible to us because they don't like us! They're **MEAN**

and **CRUEL**

and **REVOLTING!'**

'Now, now,' said Mr Lovely, taking off his straw boater and fanning himself with it, 'remember the Lovely Code, my dear! Everybody is lovely underneath! If our neighbours have tipped their bins over the hedge . . . again . . . well, I'm sure it was just an accident.'

The problem with being so lovely all the time was that Mr Lovely was simply unable to understand that some people are just twits.

THE TWITS NEXT DOOR

But the problem with being a kid, as you may have noticed, is that grown-ups don't listen to you when they really should.

Tumble rolled her eyes. 'Our neighbours are **TWITS,**' she told her dad. 'And we'll prove it to you.'

Back in the tree house after breakfast, Tumble and her brother held a meeting.

'Mum and Dad just don't understand,' she told Ruff. 'They have this idea that everybody is lovely.'

'I know,' said Ruff sadly. 'They're really not properly equipped for the modern world.'

'Well, we'll have to help them,' decided Tumble. 'We will PROVE that those Twits next door don't have a lovely bone in their whole bodies. We must go on a mission to gather evidence.'

'Oooh, cool,' said Ruff, who loved missions.

'It'll be dangerous,' warned Tumble, looking out of the window at the Twits' house. 'Who knows what that pair of **FUNGUS-RIDDEN FUDGE STICKS** get up to in there.'

'I bet it's haunted,' said Ruff. 'There're probably **VAMPIRES IN THE ATTIC.**'

'Or, like, a whole room full of **SNAKES,**' said Tumble, her eyes shining with excitement.

'Or a **BRAIN-EATING ZOMBIE** that they keep as a pet,' added Ruff. 'Let's go and find out!'

They crawled carefully out along the branch that stretched across the end of Mr and Mrs Twit's garden. Tumble had a coil of rope slung over her shoulder, and when they were above a thick patch of thistles she tied this to the branch and the twins slid down, immediately disappearing into the undergrowth.

'This is better than our garden, anyway, now Mum and Dad have made it so *lovely*,' whispered Ruff as they wriggled on their tummies towards the Twits' back door.

They were both pricked by brambles and stung by nettles, but neither of them cared — it was all too exciting.

'Almost there,' said Tumble after a while. Then she

wrinkled up her nose. **'WHATEVER IS THAT**

STENCH?' she asked.

The stink that was emerging from the kitchen was, indeed, truly horrifying because on the day the twins had decided to begin their investigations Mrs Twit had been busy in the kitchen cooking one of her specialities, Egg and Giblet Soup. If you don't know what giblets are, they are the parts of a chicken that usually get pulled out and thrown away before it is roasted. They are brown and purple and smell and taste pretty nasty. But the Twits loved them. In fact, they liked to keep the giblets and throw the rest of the chicken away. Mrs Twit used them to make a watery soup with boiled eggs floating in it. And she preferred the eggs to be very slightly rotten. She claimed it gave them more flavour.

Egg and Giblet Soup is pretty

HORRIFYING.

But not as horrifying as the noise Mr Twit made

while eating it. It was a **BUBBLING,**

SLURPING,

SLOSHING sound

that would make your stomach turn if you were within half a mile of him. As he ate, he used his beard like a sieve to filter out some of the giblet particles, then stuck out his tongue with a slimy **SPLAT** to search for them. And so, when Ruff and Tumble crept up to the back door, which had been left open to let a bit of light inside, they were greeted by the smell and sound of Egg and Giblet Soup.

'Lovely . . .

SPHLLLLLRP . . .

drop of soup . . .

SLSSsSSsSSPH . . . Mrs Twit,'

Mr Twit was saying through a mouthful of rancid egg and chicken unmentionables. He was sitting at the kitchen table with his back to the twins, so they were able to sneak right up to the door without being seen.

'Did you remember to do the bins?' said Mrs Twit, who was sitting opposite.

'**SHCHLOOoOOOOP** . . . yers,' said Mr Twit, sounding satisfied. He let out a small burp. 'I tipped all that 'ORRIBLE STINKING REFUSE right into their flower bed.' He rubbed his hands together with a smirk.

Ruff pulled a notebook from his pocket and noted down the following:

Wednesday, 11.23 a.m., we witnessed Mr Twit confessing to smelly bin crime.

He gave Tumble a nod. Evidence had been gathered.

'Let's try to get inside,' whispered his sister. 'See what else we can find out.'

When they'd finished their stinky soup, Mr and Mrs Twit got up to dump their bowls in the sink, which was already piled high with dirty dishes. Ruff and Tumble took their chance and raced silently behind them, through the kitchen and up the stairs. They spent the rest of the morning searching for more evidence, but the Twits' horrible plans were never written down.

'This is hopeless,' said Ruff after a while. 'There's nothing in here except a lot of mess.'

At that moment they heard stompy footsteps.

'QUICK!' said Tumble. 'Don't let them catch us! In the wardrobe!'

The twins darted into the wardrobe and closed the door just as Mrs Twit reached the top of the stairs.

Unfortunately for Ruff and Tumble the wardrobe was exactly where Mrs Twit was heading. She had come upstairs to fetch a coat, ready to tend to her thistle patches. But when she opened the wardrobe door she was startled to find two very similar-looking children inside staring back at her. Mrs Twit let out a long yowl like a scorched seagull and collapsed on to the bedroom floor. Ruff and Tumble, terrified, screamed right back at her.

'What is it? What's going on?' yelled Mr Twit from downstairs, hearing the yelp and the thump.

'DEMONS!'

screamed Mrs Twit. 'There's **DEMONS IN THE WARDROBE! WARDROBE DEMONS!'**

Mr Twit rushed upstairs.

'They're not demons, you daft washbasin!' he snarled, peeking nervously round the bedroom door. 'It's worse than that . . . it's **CHILDREN!'**

'YEEEARCH!'

yelled Mrs Twit in disgust, fumbling for her thwacking stick.

The twins, desperate to escape from this foul couple, leaped out of the wardrobe and darted under the closest bed.

'POKE 'EM OUT!'

urged Mr Twit, as Mrs Twit got down on to her tummy, thrusting her stick beneath the bed like a snooker cue. **'WE'LL CATCH 'EM AND BAKE 'EM INTO A LOVELY PIE!'**

Ruff and Tumble had not expected their evidence-gathering mission to end like this. They dodged back and forth beneath the saggy old bed, waiting for a chance to make a break for it. Mrs Twit's thwacking stick smacked into the leg of the bed and she loosened her grip for a split second. It was all they needed. The twins shot out from beneath the bed and made for the door. Mr Twit tried to stop them, but they dropped to the floor and **SKIDDED** across the floorboards, SLIDING

neatly between his legs and **GALLOPING** away
down the stairs.

By the time the Twits had made their way
downstairs in pursuit, the twins had raced through the
garden (gaining several more nettle stings), climbed
back up the rope and were safely hidden in the tree
house. They peered out of the window as Mr and Mrs
Twit searched through the nettles for them, howling
with rage.

'That settles it,' said Tumble. 'They are horrible twits and we're going to have to prove it.'

But what she didn't realize was that the Twits' campaign to get rid of the Lovelies was just getting started. Bins over the hedge had only been the beginning. There were far more terrible plots just round the corner . . .

CHAPTER NINE

HAIRY CAKES

'I know what'll fix those horrible Lovelies,' said Mr Twit to Mrs Twit the following day. 'I've got a very clever plan.'

He disappeared into his workshed and for the next hour the sounds of sawing, hammering and sloshing drifted across the garden. Sometime later Mr Twit emerged holding a large wooden sign. The sign had the following words written on it:

FREE PUPPIES

'Free puppies?' said Mrs Twit, looking confused. 'Free them from what?'

'**NO, NO, NO,** you poodle-brained nitwit,' replied Mr Twit. 'It means puppies what are free!'

'Oh!' Mrs Twit clapped her hands. 'Puppies what are free!'

'Yers!' replied Mr Twit. 'And when I put this sign outside that 'orrible house, everybody will turn up wanting a free puppy! And those Lovelies will have a garden full of people! Trampling all over their nice lawn and getting furious when they find out there aren't really any puppies!'

'Brilliant!' said Mrs Twit.

'Yers,' agreed Mr Twit smugly. 'It is, isn't it? I have an unusually brilliant brain today. This plot is one of my best yet.'

And, dragging the sign behind him, he crept on all fours out of the garden gate and propped it up against the hedge at the front of Mr and Mrs Lovely's house. Then he crawled back, and Mr and Mrs Twit waited for the plan to work.

You won't be surprised to hear that, as soon as they saw a large sign saying FREE PUPPIES, lots of people began to swarm through the Lovely family's front gate. Before long there was a large excited crowd on their front lawn. Many of them were indeed standing on the immaculate flower beds.

Mr Twit chuckled as he watched them gather. 'Now watch! Any minute now they will turn on those silly Lovelies when they find out there ain't no puppies. They'll attack them and smush them into goo!'

In the tree house, Ruff and Tumble had watched the whole scene unfold. They had seen Mr Twit stomping to his workshed and emerging with the FREE PUPPIES sign.

'He's trying to make Mum and Dad unpopular!' raged Ruff. 'Free puppies? They don't have any puppies to give people!'

'Come on,' said Tumble. 'Let's go and help!'

They **SCRAMBLED DOWN** the tree and raced into the house. But no help was needed. Mr and Mrs Lovely already had the situation well in hand.

When Mr Lovely had heard the crowd outside, he had thrown open the front door.

'HELLO there!' he cried. 'My goodness, what a lot of lovely people! What can we do for you today?'

'We've come for the puppies!' shouted several voices.

'Puppies?' repeated Mrs Lovely, joining her husband at the door. 'Whatever do you mean, *puppies*?'

Somebody went to fetch the sign and showed it to them.

'Oh dear, dear, dear,' said Mr Lovely, smiling widely. 'What's happened here? I rather think we've been the victim of a little prank, Mrs Lovely!'

'How hilariously funny!' said Mrs Lovely, pressing her hands to her face in delight. 'I love jokes!'

'We don't have any puppies for you,' Mr Lovely told the people, and there was a loud groan.

Behind the hedge, Mr Twit **CACKLED.** 'Now they'll turn on them!' he croaked.

'But I think I can promise you something just as nice as a puppy!' Mr Lovely went on. 'Mrs Lovely, let's open the Lovely Bus!'

'Oh **YES!**' replied Mrs Lovely. 'You wonderful

guests can be the very first people to try out my brand-new invention!'

She rushed to the bus, climbed in and opened the hatch.

'Here you all are!' she said, producing a small bottle of bright yellow liquid. 'I've been working on this for some time! It's a drink called Nice Pop. Have a try!'

NICE POPS: this fizzy drink is one of Mrs Lovely's most amazing inventions. It contains a lot of bubbles, so when you take a big sip it's impossible not to burp. But, thanks to the secret ingredient, you will burp out a lovely compliment about somebody nearby.

Mrs Lovely handed the Nice Pop to a man at the front. He opened the bottle and took a sip. The drink was very cold and very delicious and **VERY, VERY FIZZY.** The man swallowed a large mouthful while the crowd watched him expectantly.

And then, all of a sudden, he let out a

GIGANTIC
BURP

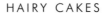

But not just a normal burp. A burp with words in it.
A word-burp if you like.

'YOU HAVE A LOVELY GARDEN,'
burped the man.

'Why, thank you!' said Mrs Lovely. 'What a very
NICE thing to say!'

Nice Pop was a fantastic invention. Mrs Lovely
handed out bottles to everyone and, within a few
minutes, the garden was full of people burping out
kind phrases to each other.

'I LIKE YOUR HAIR!'

'YOU HAVE BEAUTIFUL EYES!'

'YOUR HAT MAKES ME HAPPY!'

'THIS IS THE GREENEST LAWN I'VE EVER SEEN!'

(This burp was a particularly large and long one.)

Mr and Mrs Twit gawped from across the hedge, their mouths open. They couldn't understand why anyone would actually be kind to a load of strangers who'd flooded into their garden.

'We shall have to try something a little more cunning,' said Mr Twit, scratching his head.

'Leave it to me,' said Mrs Twit. 'I have an excellent trick, far better than your silly plan, you daft coot. Those puppies have given me a very clever idea.'

★

That very afternoon Mrs Twit marched off into town with her shopping bag over her arm. The town was busy because the big Springtime Parade was taking place the following weekend. Mrs Twit walked past shopkeepers cleaning their windows and workers climbing ladders to string bunting along the main street. But she didn't pay attention to any of it. She headed straight for one particular shop, which was a dog-grooming parlour called **THE LAUNDRO-MUTT**. Inside, Mrs Twit could see several dogs being washed and having their fur clipped. She slipped down an alleyway that led to the rear of the shop. Near the back door stood a large black bin that was full to the top with the dog hair that had been swept up from the floor of the Laundro-Mutt. Chuckling, Mrs Twit scooped up handfuls of the hair and stuffed it into her shopping bag.

Back at home, Mrs Twit set to work in the kitchen. She put eggs, milk and flour into a large mixing bowl. But whereas a normal baker would add chocolate chips or something else delicious, this batty baker poured in a huge amount of dog hair.

'What are you making?' asked Mr Twit from the doorway. 'It looks like cakes! You're never going to drive those neighbours away with cakes.'

'I will with *these* cakes,' Mrs Twit told him, holding up her wooden spoon. 'They're very special **HAIRY** cakes! They'll be the most disgusting thing those horrible Lovelies have ever tasted!'

Once the hairy cakes had been baked, Mrs Twit iced them with a very special icing that she had made by mixing washing powder and dirty bathwater. Then she placed several of them on a tray.

'Come on, Mr Twit,' she said. 'Let's leave these on their doorstep, then sit back and watch the fun.'

The Twits crept next door with the tray of hairy cakes. They placed them **SILENTLY** on the front doorstep and turned to leave. But standing behind them were Ruff and Tumble with their hands on their hips.

'And just **WHAT** do you think you are doing?' asked Ruff.

'Nothing,' said Mrs Twit, grinning wickedly. 'Just leaving some, er, nice, tasty cakes for you and your mum and dad.'

'Is that so?' asked Tumble suspiciously.

The twins had heard wicked laughter coming from the Twits' kitchen and suspected that they had been cooking up something revolting.

'MUM! DAD!' shouted Tumble suddenly. **'OUR NEIGHBOURS ARE HERE!'**

'Oh,' said Mrs Twit in a panic. 'No need to bother your parents, youngsterlings.'

But she was too late. The front door opened.

'Why, hello, neighbours!' said Mr Lovely. 'Look, Mrs Lovely – our next-door neighbours have come to visit!'

'Good day, Mr and Mrs Twit!' said Mrs Lovely, also coming to the door. 'And it looks like you've brought us something rather tasty!'

'OOOOH, CAKES!' agreed Mr Lovely. 'My very favourite!'

Mr and Mrs Twit were stunned into silence. They

had been hoping to leave the disgusting cakes secretly and creep away.

Tumble had an idea. 'As Mr and Mrs Twit are our guests,' she said, 'don't you think they should have the first bite of these lovely cakes?'

Mrs Twit shook her head. 'Oh, **NO NO NO,'** she mumbled.

'OH YES, YES, YES!' said Ruff, realizing what his sister was doing. 'Tumble is absolutely right!'

'OPEN WIDE!' insisted Tumble, grabbing two cakes from the tray and holding them up. Both Mr and Mrs Twit opened their mouths to try to refuse. But before they could speak, Tumble had jammed a cake into each of their faces.

'There you are!' she said. 'We couldn't accept your lovely gift without sharing with our neighbours, could we?'

She winked at Ruff, delighted to be quite literally giving the Twits a taste of their own medicine.

Both Twits had no choice but to chew. The texture of a cake full of dog hair is something that we hope you'll never have to experience. It's both **CLAGGY** and **TICKLY**. The hairs get caught between your teeth and make you cough. And let's not forget the washing-powder icing, which tasted like a soapy nightmare.

Mr and Mrs Twit's eyes both grew as large as saucers. They made peculiar **GAGGING, CHOKING**

noises. And then, mouths still full, they both turned tail and ran back towards their own house, taking the tray of hairy cakes with them in their panic.

'How strange,' said Mrs Lovely, watching them go with genuine concern. 'Perhaps they remembered something very important they have to do.'

'Still, it was lovely of them to bring us cakes, even if we didn't get to eat them,' said Mr Lovely.

'DON'T YOU GET IT?!' raged Tumble. 'They made those cakes disgusting **ON PURPOSE!**

They are

HORRIBLE

TWITS!'

'Oh, I don't think so, dearest,' said Mr Lovely mildly. 'Remember, everybody is lovely underneath!' Then he closed the door.

★

'BLEEERRRGGGHHH!'

groaned Mr Twit, rushing into their kitchen and scrubbing his tongue with the washing-up brush. 'Those cakes were revolting!'

'They were SUPPOSED to be revolting!' said Mrs Twit, crouching down on all fours and spitting out what looked like a cat's hairball on to the rug. 'Those rotten Lovelies! We're **NEVER** going to get rid of them!'

'Oh yes, we are,' said Mr Twit, picking dog hairs out from under his tongue. 'We just need to be even more clever about it!'

CHAPTER TEN

THE TIGER TAMER'S
TAME TIGER

By now Ruff and Tumble had plenty of evidence about the terrible **TWITTERY** that had been going on. Ruff had been jotting all kinds of details down in his notebook about the bins over the hedge, the FREE PUPPIES sign and the cakes full of dog hair. He now had a list of all the awful tricks that had been played on Mr and Mrs Lovely. Unfortunately, though, the twins' parents kept insisting that Mr and Mrs Twit – like everybody else – must be **LOVELY UNDERNEATH**.

'Why can't you get this into your heads? Those horrible Twits next door are trying to get rid of us!'

said Tumble to her father over breakfast.

'Don't be silly,' Mr Lovely said.

'It's true!' insisted Ruff. 'He tipped the bins over the hedge!'

'People don't do that kind of thing,' broke in Mrs Lovely.

'They tried to poison you!' added Tumble. 'We saw her coming back to the house with a bag of furry stuff, grinning like an **EVIL MANIAC!'**

'Children, children,' said Mr Lovely soothingly, 'I'm sure you've been playing a very imaginative game up there in the tree. But real people don't behave like that! Have you forgotten item three?'

He pointed to the embroidered Lovely Code on the wall.

*Everybody is
lovely underneath*

'Well, the Twits aren't lovely, on the outside OR underneath,' Tumble told her parents. 'And you'll work it out for yourselves in the end. Or at least I hope you will, before they do something even more evil.'

'And when you do,' said Ruff as he followed his sister through the door, 'be sure to let us know. We can help you get **REVENGE.**

MWA HA HA!'

'Now that wouldn't be true to the Lovely Code, would it?' shouted Mrs Lovely after the twins. 'Remember item one: be lovely at all times to everybody!'

★

Next door, Mr and Mrs Twit were sitting opposite each other in their dank old armchairs, plotting away like anything. They had no intention of being lovely to anybody, **EVER.**

'What if we put a hose through their letterbox and filled their house with water?' suggested Mrs Twit.

'They'd probably enjoy it,' replied Mr Twit, scowling. 'They're the kind of people what are always WASHING. They LIKE water.' Mr Twit never drank water unless it had been made into beer first.

'We could put a great big bat in their fridge?' suggested Mrs Twit.

'YOU'RE a great big bat,' retorted Mr Twit rudely. 'Anyway, bats like cold, dark places. It would probably live in the fridge quite happily.'

'Until someone opened the door,' Mrs Twit pointed out. 'Then it would FLAP right in their face.'

'We're not thinking big enough,' said Mr Twit. 'What we need is something that will get rid of those Lovelies once and for all.'

'Something that will get rid of them,' agreed Mrs Twit, stroking her pimply chin thoughtfully.

'Something that would **EAT THEM ALL UP** and get them to scarper,' decided Mr Twit.

Mrs Twit clicked her knobbly fingers. 'I know! What about a tiger? We could let a TIGER loose in their house! That would eat 'em up all right!'

'You crumbly piecrust,' said Mr Twit with a snort. 'Where on earth are we going to get hold of a tiger?'

'We could borrow one from the Tiger Tamer.'

'Oh yeah,' Mr Twit replied, annoyed. 'I hadn't thought of him.'

Once upon a time Mr and Mrs Twit had worked in a circus. This was a long time ago, when circuses had performing animals who were forced to do tricks and stand up on podiums and all that kind of nonsense. The Twits had been in charge of training the monkeys, which they had very much enjoyed because, like all true twits, they enjoyed being mean to animals.

The Twits had only kept in touch with one person from their circus days. His name was Herbert Slobgollion and his job was to train the tigers. We say 'train' but, in fact, what he used to do was hit the tigers with sticks until they did what he wanted. The Twits' monkey-training technique had been very similar, which is why they had stayed in contact. They had a shared interest in hitting animals with sticks.

Herbert Slobgollion had also left the circus, but he lived nearby and the Twits happened to know that he had taken several tigers with him when he retired. And so, the very next morning, they set off to borrow one.

The Tiger Tamer's house was a **LARGE RAMSHACKLE** building on the other side of town. It was surrounded by a huge garden for the tigers to roam around and a high fence to keep the tigers in. There were sturdy, solid gates at the front of the property and Mrs Twit knocked on these with her stick. There was a startled **ROAR** from behind the gate.

'That one sounds good and hungry,' said Mrs Twit in a satisfied tone. 'Sounds like it would EAT those Lovelies right up in one gulp.'

After a moment one of the gates opened and Herbert Slobgollion the Tiger Tamer stuck his head out. He had a round red face like a tomato with a small thin moustache stuck on the front like a furry worm. He wore a bright red jacket and an old top hat with teeth marks in it.

'Mr and Mrs Twit!' said the Tiger Tamer in surprise. 'I haven't seen you in a while! Come in, come in!'

The Twits squeezed through the gate and Slobgollion shut it behind them.

'Hit any animals with sticks lately?' he asked politely, in the same tone that you or I might say, 'Been on any nice holidays recently?'

'I almost got a bird the other day,' said Mrs Twit. 'But it flew off too quickly.'

'What a shame!' said Slobgollion. 'It's the only way to make these animals learn, you know. Spare the stick and spoil the tiger, that's what I say! These animals don't know what's good for 'em – but we do!'

'STICKS!' agreed Mrs Twit, swishing her own through the air.

Slobgollion grinned. 'Right in one! Anyway,' he

went on, 'enough of this pleasant chit-chat. What can I do for you both on this fine day?'

'We'd like to borrow a tiger, please,' said Mr Twit. 'The fiercest one you've got. One that will gobble up a whole couple and both their horrible kids. Have you got any really, really fierce ones?'

'All my tigers are fierce,' said Slobgollion proudly. 'I'd be out of a job if they weren't. Have a look!'

Mr and Mrs Twit peered around. The Tiger Tamer's garden was like a small jungle. There were high trees and large patches of tall grass. A tiger's stripy coat is especially designed to hide in this kind of place, so the Twits were unable to spot anything.

'Where are they?' asked Mr Twit finally.

'I'll flush 'em out for you,' replied the Tiger Tamer. And, fetching a big stick that was propped up near his front door, he disappeared into the undergrowth. There was a **SMACK,** followed by a **ROAR,** and a large tiger leaped out from the tall grass and looked at the Twits angrily.

'What about this one?' asked Slobgollion. 'Fierce enough for you?'

'Will he eat our neighbours?' Mrs Twit wanted to know.

'Oh yes,' Slobgollion replied airily. 'Absolutely. With ease. He hasn't been fed since . . . well, I can't remember when, to be honest. He'll eat up your neighbours, no problem.'

'And their horrible annoying kids?' Mr Twit added.

'Before they can say, "Aargh, no, no, no, I'm being eaten!"' Slobgollion reassured him.

'Lovely,' said Mr Twit, looking at the tiger slightly nervously. 'Can we borrow him, then?'

'You'll be doing me a favour,' said Slobgollion. 'If he eats your neighbours, I won't have to go out and buy tiger food for him. Two neighbours and their kids? He won't need dinner for a fortnight. I'll go and get his lead.'

The tiger had a large leather collar round his neck

and Slobgollion fastened a thick lead to this, handing the end to Mrs Twit.

'Just threaten him with your stick if he misbehaves,' he told her. 'He don't like the stick,' he added, 'do yer, pal?'

He waved his own stick. The tiger gave a small growl at this and the Twits jumped back.

'Come on, now,' Mrs Twit told the tiger, pulling it by the lead towards the gate. 'Come with us. We've got some nice neighbours for you to eat. Tasty neighbours! **YUM YUM!'**

The tiger, thinking to itself that anything was better than staying in this garden and being hit with sticks, followed her. And if you're wondering why it didn't eat Mr and Mrs Twit, you need to ask yourself: would you?

It's not every day you see a dirty pair of twits walking a tiger down the main street. And, before long, a trail of children had gathered behind the Twits as they walked home. Mrs Twit had to turn round every so often and shoo them away with her stick, but the children were so fascinated by the sight of a real live tiger on a lead that they kept coming back again. It was only when Mr Twit threatened to set the tiger loose that they eventually gave up and went home.

'I'll set him on you!' he told the frightened children, moving his hand towards the collar. 'He's a fast runner too! You'd better rush home before you all get eaten!'

Screaming, the children turned tail and ran off.

'Now,' Mrs Twit told the tiger as they approached Mr and Mrs Lovely's house, 'it's time for you to do some NEIGHBOUR EATING!'

The tiger let out a very hungry-sounding

GROWL.

CHAPTER ELEVEN

THE TIGER WHO CAME TO BREAKFAST

'How are we going to get the tiger into the house?' asked Mr Twit as he dragged the tiger towards the Lovelies' front gate.

'I've thought of that,' Mrs Twit said reassuringly. 'I've thought of my cleverest plan yet.'

She rummaged in her pocket and pulled out a large label made of brown cardboard. On this, she had written in her spidery handwriting:

POOR LOST CAT
Please take me into your home
(I know I look big but I am a real cat.)
(Honestly not a fierce hungry tiger or anything.)
Thank you.

'BRILLIANT!' said Mr Twit. 'Those soft-hearted softy heads won't be able to resist!'

'And they won't ever suspect it's really a tiger,' added Mrs Twit smugly, 'because it says on its label that it isn't! I'm a GENIUS!'

Mr Twit didn't think that Mrs Twit was a genius. He thought she was a **FOUL, NAGGING, SHRIEKING** pain in the posterior. But he was so keen to get rid of Mr and Mrs Lovely that he decided not to say so on this occasion. Making a mental note to play an especially mean trick on her as soon as possible, he helped Mrs Twit attach the label to the tiger's collar before leading it to the door of the Lovely house and telling it to **'SIT!'** The tiger, which was just relieved to be having a day out instead of living in a garden where Herbert Slobgollion kept hitting it with a stick, obeyed.

Mrs Twit rapped sharply on the door with her stick, then said to Mr Twit, 'Now hide, quick!'

The Twits scurried off behind a tree like two giant dirty mice and waited.

When Mrs Lovely answered the door, she was fairly surprised to find a tiger sitting there. Well, you would be, wouldn't you? It's not something that happens every day, unless you subscribe to a mail-order tiger subscription. And we're not even sure they exist, although they should.

'*Poor . . . lost . . . cat*,' said Mrs Lovely, reading the cardboard label.

At this moment the twins rushed up behind her. They had been watching as usual from the tree house and had seen Mr and Mrs Twit dragging the tiger down the road by its lead.

'IT'S A TRAP!' yelled Tumble.

'I'm fairly sure it's a tiger,' replied Mrs Lovely calmly.

'IT'S A TIGER TRAP!' said Ruff. 'Those mean Twits left it there! They're trying to get us eaten up! It's a fierce hungry tiger!'

'Mmm,' said Mrs Lovely. She and the tiger looked at each other. Animals are very perceptive. Immediately the tiger could tell that it was meeting a kind and caring person. Mrs Lovely was also perceptive – at least, perceptive enough to work out that this was definitely not a cat like the label said. But, being a lovely person, she loved all animals – and this one looked particularly underfed and badly cared for.

'I think you'd better come in,' Mrs Lovely told the tiger, ignoring the twins' protests and opening the door wide.

Once the front door had closed, Mr and Mrs Twit emerged from behind the tree.

'BRILLIANT!' said Mrs Twit, her knuckles cracking like fireworks as she rubbed her hands together. **'I AM COMPLETELY BRILLIANT!'**

'All right, all right,' grumbled Mr Twit, annoyed that her plan seemed to be working better than any of his. 'Come on – let's go home and wait for the

SCREAMS.'

Back at their house, the Twits dragged their chairs near the front door, which they left open so they could hear what was happening. They sat down, looking as if they were waiting for their favourite TV programme to start.

Mr Twit had poured himself an extra-large mug of beer.

'Any moment now,' he said, tilting his head to one side and cupping a hand behind his ear to hear better.

'Why hasn't there been any screaming yet?' said Mrs Twit half an hour later.

'It's probably stalking them around the house,' growled Mr Twit, enjoying this idea enormously. 'Biding its time. They're probably trying to hide in the wardrobes, but it'll sniff 'em out in the end. They're excellent sniffers, tigers. Some of the best. And then –'

'It'll EAT 'em all up!' finished Mrs Twit, rocking back and forth in her chair with glee. 'Then no Lovelies ever again! And nobody will ever dare try to live next door to us.'

TWO HOURS LATER . . .

'Stupid tiger,' said Mr Twit.

'I thought you said it was biding its time,' said Mrs Twit.

'Well, it needs to do a little less biding and a lot more **GOBBLING** up,' said Mr Twit, yawning. 'I'm getting tired.'

And after a while both Twits fell asleep in their chairs. They slept the whole night through until at dawn they were jolted awake by the sound of screaming coming from the house next door.

Mr and Mrs Twit rushed excitedly into the garden.

'It's happening! It's happening!' said Mr Twit. 'Hurry up, Mrs Twit, or you'll miss it!'

He led the way to the hedge and stood on a rusty old bucket, ready to survey the horror.

He was hoping to see the tiger eating the entire Lovely family for breakfast. However, you'll be pleased to hear that isn't what he saw. What he saw instead was this:

The tiger was giving Ruff and Tumble a ride around the garden on its back. The twins were screaming with excitement, which is the noise the

Twits had heard, of course. Screams of delight rather than screams of pain — the Twits' least favourite of all the screams.

Mr and Mrs Lovely were watching from the kitchen door, beaming, while Mrs Lovely tapped a tambourine and sang a little song that went:

Ride that tiger,
Ride that tiger,
All around the garden.

'Ah, good morning, Mr Twit!' said Mr Lovely, catching sight of the mean, bearded face peeking over the hedge. 'You won't believe what's happened! This poor hungry tiger wandered into our house yesterday. It must have escaped from one of those terrible circuses!'

'Why haven't you been **EATED UP?'** bellowed Mr Twit before he could stop himself.

Mr Lovely, who believed the best of everybody, thought he was just being a concerned neighbour. 'Oh, don't worry, my dear chap!' he said, smiling. 'The stripy little fellow had obviously been mistreated! As soon as we gave him something to eat and a few cuddles, he felt much better.'

There are not many words that anger Mr Twit more than the word **'CUDDLE'.** To him, it's one of the most disgusting, rudest words you could possibly say. At the thought of Mr Lovely feeding the tiger and then cuddling it, Mr Twit's face went an angry shade of red. His whole body began to **SHAKE** – so much so, in fact, that his foot went right through the rusty bucket and he dropped out of sight behind the hedge.

'What happened?' Mrs Twit wanted to know. 'What's he talking about **CUDDLES** for?'

'Don't use that revolting word!' Mr Twit told her, stomping back to the house.

There was a bucket round one of his ankles so he went STOMP, CLANG, STOMP, CLANG.

He threw himself back down in his chair and reached for his beer. He intended to sit there until he had made a new plan – a plan that would get rid of the Lovelies once and for all.

The tiger, meanwhile, settled in very nicely at the Lovely house. Like any animal, it had only been fierce when it was under attack. Slobgollion had spent most of his time hitting it with a stick, so naturally this had made it very bad-tempered. Mr and Mrs Lovely, however, showered it with affection and large bowls of Mr Lovely's special beef stew. Tigers are excellent tree climbers and it found the tree house almost straight away. There it lived with Ruff and Tumble, curling up at the foot of their beds each night, looking for all the world like the overlarge cat that Mrs Twit had tried to pretend it was.

The twins knew perfectly well that the Twits had left the tiger on their doorstep, hoping it would attack and eat them. They had added this to Ruff's evidence notebook. But they were too excited to have a new pet tiger to worry too much about it.

★

Mr Twit spent the rest of that day in his chair, still with the bucket round his ankle. He thought so hard that his beard began to **VIBRATE** and pieces of food fell on to his trouser legs. He thought so hard that his ears went bright red and **WIGGLED** from side to side. He thought so hard that his eyes **BULGED** out of his head like two hard-boiled

eggs being squeezed through a keyhole. And then, finally, at precisely 6.54 p.m., he clicked his fingers.

'I'VE GOT IT!' said Mr Twit.

'Well, put some ointment on it then,' replied Mrs Twit, who was sitting opposite him thinking about clowns.

'No, you soggy pudding!' scolded Mr Twit. 'I haven't got THAT again. I mean, I've got IT! **IT!**

A PLAN!

A PLOT!

A CUNNING TRICK!'

Mrs Twit jiggled in her chair with excitement. **'OOOH!'**

'And this time it will WORK!' boasted Mr Twit. 'We'll be free of those 'orrible LOVELIES once and for all.'

Then both Twits began to laugh with a horrible **CROAKING** sound like crows with sore throats.

CHAPTER TWELVE

THE TREE, THE CATAPULT AND THE ENORMOUS PLOT TWIST

The very next morning Mr Twit shut himself away in his workshed and began to gather materials to put his EVIL PLOT into action. He had a giant roll of extra-strong elastic called

ULTRA-SPROING
SUPER-STRETCH

(which he normally used to hold up his underpants), along with some metal cogs and levers, some rope and a great deal of wood.

'This plan,' said Mr Twit through a mouthful of nails, 'is my most brilliant and cleverest yet. It cannot possibly fail.'

He spent the whole day in the workshed,

HAMMERING,
SAWING
AND GLUING.

When dusk had fallen, he waited patiently until the Lovely twins and their tiger climbed into the tree house and went to sleep. And then he really went to work.

Mr Twit worked all night. He climbed **UP** and **DOWN** the Big Dead Tree. He used his ladder to TIE things to the roof of the house. He worked harder than he had ever worked in his whole life. Finally, as dawn broke the next morning, he was ready to put his horrible plan into action.

When Ruff and Tumble woke up, they went to the tree-house window as usual to see what was going on over at the Twits' house.

Tumble peered through the binoculars. 'What's that?' she said.

'What's what?' asked Ruff.

'There's something up in that old tree,' said Tumble, handing him the binoculars. 'Look!'

Ruff looked and, sure enough, there was a large bundle of paper lying on the thickest branch of the Big Dead Tree. It was a very high branch, right at the top of the ladder, which was leaning against the trunk. It had writing on and he strained his eyes to read it.

'E . . . VIL . . . PLANS . . .' read Ruff. **'CLA . . . SSI . . . FIED.'**

'Evil plans!' repeated Tumble. 'Classified! You know what this means? Those horrible Twits have left their secret plans up in the tree! If we show them to Mum and Dad, they'll HAVE to believe us! Come on!'

The twins edged out along the branch and

SLID
DOWN
THE
ROPE into the Twits' garden. They crept through the tall nettles and thistles until they reached the Big Dead Tree. The garden appeared to be deserted.

'Those Twits must still be fast asleep,' said Tumble softly. 'I think the coast is clear! Let's go!'

Ruff and Tumble darted out from the cover of the thistles, and raced up the ladder. But when they reached the bundle of papers marked **EVIL PLANS – CLASSIFIED**, something unexpected and terrible happened. The ladder was suddenly snatched away from beneath them.

'PAHAHAAAAA,'

said Mr Twit, who had been hiding among the thistles like a sneaky badger. 'That'll fix you! You're stranded in the tree! It's far too high to jump! Do you really think I'd be so stupid as to write down all my evil plans in a folder with EVIL PLANS on the front? I don't need to write them down – they're all up here!' He tapped the side of his head. 'And now you are **TRAPPED!** Caught in my cleverest ever **PLOT.**'

'Put that ladder back!' yelled Tumble furiously.

'SHAN'T!' retorted Mr Twit.

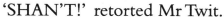

'Our mum and dad will come to rescue us!' said Ruff.

'Oh, I'm counting on it,' said Mr Twit gloatingly. 'And when they do . . . they'll get a VERY nasty surprise.'

He pointed to a pile of leaves just in front of the tree.

'That's my hidden catapult,' Mr Twit explained, pointing to the lengths of thick elastic that emerged from the leaves. 'And when they come to rescue you, I shall **SPRING THE TRAP** and your precious parents will be **LAUNCHED INTO SPACE** and you'll never see them again!'

Mr Twit had indeed spent the night building a gigantic catapult.

The lengths of ULTRA-SPROING SUPER-STRETCH were tied to the roof of the house, and led to a hidden platform beneath the leaves. When Mr Twit activated his trap, this platform would be fired upwards with enormous force, sending anyone standing on it flying high into the air.

'You really are a horrible, mean twit, aren't you?' said Tumble furiously.

'Yesss,' said Mr Twit, 'I am. I am also an extremely clever plotter-er. Much cleverer-er than you. I have outfoxed you like a CUNNIN' FOX! Now stay there until your parents come looking for you. And then . . . you can WAVE THEM GOODBYE as I pull this lever and

BOING THEM INTO ORBIT.'

With that, cackling, he retreated back into his house and slammed the door.

'Is it done?' asked Mrs Twit eagerly.

'It is,' said Mr Twit, smacking his lips with excitement. 'Now we just have to wait.'

From outside he could hear the twins shouting for help, but the Big Dead Tree was too far away for their parents to hear them.

Mr and Mrs Twit decided to fill the time while they waited with a game of Angry Alphabet. The rules are simple: you take it in turn to go through the alphabet thinking of insults beginning with each letter and shouting them at each other. We don't recommend this as a game to play with your own family because it can get rather offensive. But the Twits, who hated each other, loved it.

'Ant brain!' yelled Mr Twit at his wife.

'Bottom face!' she screeched in reply.

'Carrot nose!'

'Droopy dinosaur!'

Mr Twit got stuck for a second, but then continued: 'Egg!'

'What's insulting about an egg?' Mrs Twit wanted to know. 'I like eggs.'

'You're a rotten stinking old egg what's been down a dirty toilet for a fortnight,' Mr Twit clarified.

'That's better,' she said approvingly. 'Five points. And you are a filthy fudge-fingered, feather-brained fish face,' she added.

'Oooh, we're warming up now,' said Mr Twit. 'That was a good one. You great gorilla-gutted garage full of gorgonzola!'

Just then there came a shout from outside. 'Ruff! Tumble! WHERE ARE YOU?'

'QUIET!' shouted Mrs Twit angrily. The noise had interrupted her while she was trying to think of something really rude beginning with H.

'It's THEM!' said Mr Twit. 'It's those Lovelies! They're looking for their children! Now to finish my MASTER PLAN!'

'Horrible hairy halibut!' said Mrs Twit.

'Never mind that now!' urged Mr Twit. 'Come outside and watch me LAUNCH the Lovelies INTO SPACE!'

'OOOH,' said Mrs Twit, struggling out of her chair. 'Now that really DOES sound lovely!'

The Twits sneaked to the back door and opened it.

There, in their garden, were Mr and Mrs Lovely.

'Ruff! Tumble!' Mrs Lovely was shouting as she picked her way through the nettles. 'Where are you?'

'Over here, Mum!' shouted Ruff.

'Those Twits trapped us in the tree!' added Tumble.

'Don't be silly,' began Mrs Lovely. 'I'm sure they haven't – **YOU'RE TRAPPED IN A TREE!'** she screamed, catching sight of her children in the Big Dead Tree.

At this point something rather strange and interesting started to happen to Mrs Lovely. Something that had never happened before in her entire lovely life. She began to grow angry. Usually she was the most placid of people, but seeing her beloved twins stuck dangerously high up in a tree . . . well, it's enough to make anybody angry, isn't it? Mrs Lovely began, for the first time ever, to register on the

ANGER SCALE.

If you're not familiar with the Anger Scale, here's a quick reminder:

ANGER LEVEL	EFFECT
1. TINY ANNOYANCE	Going 'tut' quietly
2. SLIGHT ANNOYANCE	Rolling of the eyes
3. ANNOYANCE	Audible breath out through the nose
4. MILD IRRITATION	Making that horse noise with your lips
5. SLIGHT IRRITATION	Saying 'for goodness' sake' under your breath
6. IRRITATION	Saying 'for goodness' sake' out loud
7. A BIT **ANGRY**	Hopping about, stamping feet
8. REALLY **QUITE ANGRY**	Pointing of finger
9. **PROPERLY ANGRY**	Shouting, raging, possible use of bad words
10. TOTAL FURY	Brain freeze, inability to speak

Even though she was lovely, Mrs Lovely was already at **LEVEL 8.**

'DID YOU TRAP RUFF AND TUMBLE IN THAT TREE?' she asked Mr and Mrs Twit loudly.

'YES!' replied Mrs Twit with a cackle.

'Don't you want to go and RESCUE them?' suggested Mr Twit. 'The ladder's just over there,' he added, 'on the other side of that pile of leaves.'

'DON'T STEP ON THE LEAVES, MUM!' shouted Tumble. **'IT'S A TRAP!'**

'YOU'LL BE FIRED INTO SPACE!' said Ruff.

'How do they know that?' complained Mrs Twit to her husband. 'Hang on, you didn't make the classic mistake of explaining your entire evil plan to them, did you?'

'I might have done that,' admitted Mr Twit, shuffling his feet with embarrassment.

'You impossibly inch-brained idiot!' Mrs Twit told him.

'Hey! It's supposed to be my turn!' said Mr Twit, thinking for a moment that they were still playing Angry Alphabet.

Mr Lovely, in the meantime, had edged his way round the hidden catapult and was busy rescuing the twins. He grabbed the ladder, which was lying among the nettles, and began to climb towards them, feeling rather heroic.

Mrs Lovely was still looking at Mr and Mrs Twit. She was now nudging 8.5 on the Anger Scale and rising fast. 'Why did you try to trick us into standing on a giant catapult?' she asked.

'To GET RID OF YOU, of course!' replied Mr Twit.

'YES!' said Mrs Twit, poking her stick at Mrs Lovely. 'Why don't you and your family just **MOVE AWAY?** We don't want you living next door! Your horrible children make me

SICK TO
MY STOMACH!'

'But . . . but . . .' Mrs Lovely was almost speechless. But luckily not quite, because she was about to drop an enormous plot twist. 'But we've always been so LOVELY to you both!' she blurted out.

'We don't WANT you being lovely all over us!' snapped Mrs Twit, poking her stick again. 'Why did you come and live here anyway? Why can't you just LEAVE US ALONE?'

'I will TELL YOU the answer to that question!' said Mrs Lovely furiously.

'GO ON, THEN!' said Mrs Twit, never for a split second guessing what she was about to hear.

'It's because I'm your long-lost twin sister,' said Mrs Lovely.

And if this ever gets made into a film, there will be a loud piece of music here that goes

DUN-

DUN-

DUUUUNNNNN.

And if it doesn't get made into a film, you'll just have to sing the dramatic music for yourself.

CHAPTER THIRTEEN
GREAT-AUNT BISCUIT

Mrs Twit and Mrs Lovely stared at each other. Nobody spoke for quite some time.

'You're my WHAT?' screeched Mrs Twit finally.

'Your long-lost twin sister,' repeated Mrs Lovely.

'She CAN'T be your twin sister,' Mr Twit said. 'You two don't look anything like each other!'

He turned from Mrs Twit to Mrs Lovely and back again . . . and gradually an expression of wonderment began to make its way across his features, like daylight dawning across a stinky bog.

Mrs Twit's face was grumpy-looking and lined with deep frown lines. Mrs Lovely's face was open and cheerful, with laughter lines round the eyes. But when you looked really, really closely, you could see that, once upon a time, they might have been quite similar faces. Mrs Twit remembered the first time she had seen her neighbour over the garden hedge and thought she seemed strangely familiar. They were, indeed, twin sisters. But whereas one sister had spent her life with lovely thoughts that had made her face sunny and kind, the other had dwelt on mean, selfish thoughts that had made her look unhappy and cruel. And like a horrible used teabag. Or an unusually ugly mongoose.

Yes, Mrs Lovely was indeed Mrs Twit's long-lost twin sister.

DIDN'T SEE THAT ONE COMING, DID YOU?

They had been separated as babies, and Mrs Lovely had spent a great deal of time tracking down her lost sibling. The story of why they were separated is very old and very sad, but also quite long so we don't have time to go into it fully right now. But basically baby Mrs Twit was accidentally left in a large black handbag that was picked up by a doctor by mistake, and the doctor got on a train and the train got diverted . . . There isn't time for any more, but you get the idea.

'Whoa!' said Ruff – who along with Tumble was now safely down from the Big Dead Tree. 'She's your SISTER?'

'She is indeed,' replied Mrs Lovely.

'She's our AUNTIE?' called out the twins.

'I'm afraid so,' their mother replied.

'Wait a second,' said Tumble. 'Is that the reason that you never wanted to believe us when we said she was being horrible to you?'

'Well, partly, I suppose,' said Mrs Lovely.

'But also because we firmly believe that

EVERYBODY IS LOVELY UNDERNEATH,' said Mr Lovely.

'Well, about that,' said Mrs Lovely. 'I'm not actually sure I agree with the Lovely Code any more.'

'WHAT?!' said Mr Lovely, Ruff and Tumble at the same time.

Mrs Twit, meanwhile, was staring at Mrs Lovely with her mouth wide open, gaping like a pelican with mumps. Learning she had a twin sister would have been fairly monumental news for most people. But not for Mrs Twit. In case you had forgotten, she was a total twit. She also didn't like other people. She had no use for a sister, not even a long-lost twin one. It seems a shame but there you go.

'What do you want then?' she asked her sister rudely.

'What do I WANT?' asked Mrs Lovely. 'What do you mean, what do I want?'

'People always WANT something,' said Mrs Twit. 'You must have come looking for me for a reason! So what is it? Whatever it is, you can't have it,' she added quickly.

'I came here to see,' said Mrs Lovely, 'whether or not we should give you an

ENORMOUS
AMOUNT OF MONEY.'

'A what?' said Mr Twit, his eyes widening.

Mrs Twit seemed to have lost the power of speech.

'A **GIANT** FORTUNE,' said Mrs Lovely, 'that would make you **INCREDIBLY** RICH.'

'A GIANT FORTUNE?' asked Mr Twit greedily.

'Yes,' confirmed Mrs Lovely. 'A giant one. All thanks to Great–Aunt Biscuit.'

'Who on earth is THAT?' asked Mr Twit, as Mrs Twit continued to gape, which was no help at all to anybody.

Mrs Lovely told them the following story:

Once, not very long ago, there was an extremely rich old lady. Her full name was Dame Eurydice Hislop Pomfret Pomfret, but everybody in her family simply knew her as **GREAT-AUNT BISCUIT**. This was because she was the inventor of the most delicious biscuits ever: Pomfret's Lemon Whisps.

Pomfret's Lemon Whisps are the

LIGHTEST,

SWEETEST,
BUTTERIEST,
TANGIEST,

CRUMBLIEST biscuits

you have ever tasted. They melt in your mouth, leaving you feeling like a ray of citrus-scented sunshine has just passed through your brain. They also go very well with a nice cup of tea — and even if you dunk them, they don't fall to pieces. Pomfret's Lemon Whisps had made millions of people happy over the years, and they had also made Great-Aunt Biscuit a great deal of money. A really, really great deal. Like, a LOT of money. When she died at the grand old age of 103, she left this money to her family, but on one condition: it could only ever be used to make people happy.

Mrs Lovely was Great-Aunt Biscuit's favourite great-niece. And so she had been given the job of handing out this enormous fortune. She had given a huge amount to her cousin

Algernon, who ran a seal sanctuary. She had made sure that her mother-in-law, who ran a business that gave surprise birthday parties to lonely people, got a big chunk of money as well. And she had used part of the fortune to set up the Lovely Bus and fund her workshop where she invented all the things designed to give people a lovely day.

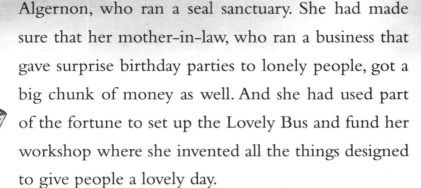

But while she had been looking through the family records after the death of Great-Aunt Biscuit, Mrs Lovely had discovered something amazing. She had found out that she had a twin sister. She discovered the story of the baby and the doctor and the train, which there still isn't time to tell you about. Excitedly Mrs Lovely began to search for her long-lost sister. *Surely*, she thought, *she must be just as lovely*. And when she found her sister, Mrs Lovely would be in a position to make her extremely rich. What could be better?

When Mrs Lovely had seen Mr and Mrs Twit for the first time, sloshing around by the pond, she had been rather shocked, but she had reminded herself of the Lovely Code. *Everybody is lovely underneath.*

But now, after seeing her twins trapped in a tree, she had decided that the Lovely Code might need a bit of an update.

When Mrs Lovely had finished telling Mrs Twit the story of Great-Aunt Biscuit, Mrs Twit rubbed her hands together with a crack of knuckles that sounded like snooker balls **CLACKING** together.

'So me and Mr Twit are about to be RICH, are we?' she gloated. 'How much money are you going to give us?'

The twins looked at each other.

'She's surely not going to give that pair of foul twits any of Great-Aunt Biscuit's money, is she?' said Tumble, looking worried. But there was no need.

'How much money am I going to give you? **NOT ONE SINGLE PENNY!**' shouted Mrs Lovely, who had now progressed to Level 9 on the Anger Scale.

'WHY?' demanded Mrs Twit.

'Because that money is to make people **HAPPY,**' said Mrs Lovely. 'And you don't make anyone happy . . . not even yourself! You and your horrible husband only like playing mean tricks on each other. You and I are the complete OPPOSITE of each other!'

'Well,' said Mrs Twit, poking her long–lost sister with the stick once again. 'You are a

JIGGLY . . .

JABBERING . . .

JAM HEAD!'

All these insults had already been in her head ready to restart the game of Angry Alphabet, so they came spilling out quite naturally.

'And YOU . . .' replied Mrs Lovely. 'YOU . . .'

The twins watched their mother in amazement. They had never seen her so angry. Surely she wasn't about to say something that wasn't lovely for the first time in her life?

'YOU . . .' continued Mrs Lovely,

'ARE A KNUCKLE-HEADED, KNOCK-KNEED, KNOBBLY KAYAK FULL OF

KANGAROO KIDNEYS!'

Mr Lovely gave a **SMALL GASP** and his legs buckled slightly.

'You're a LAZY LOVELY!' retorted Mrs Twit, glaring fiercely at her sister.

It takes some sisters years to reach the stage where they can't stand each other, but they were progressing fast. It was very impressive considering they hadn't seen each other in decades.

'You are the worst neighbours ever,' Mrs Lovely told her, 'you mean, mangy, mumbling MOO COW!'

'To be fair, she's actually very good at Angry Alphabet for a beginner,' said Mr Twit to no one in particular.

But Mrs Lovely didn't hear him. She had now reached Level 10 on the Anger Scale. 'You shall never touch

ONE
SINGLE
BRASS
FARTHING

of Great-Aunt Biscuit's fortune!'

Shaking with rage, she looked at Mr and Mrs Twit with a face as angry as a lioness that has just been told its cubs didn't get into their first choice of primary school.

'YAY!' cheered the twins, delighted to see their mild-mannered mum sticking up for herself.

'Come on, Lovely family,' said Mrs Lovely, leading her husband and the twins back towards their own house. **'THIS MEANS WAR!'**

CHAPTER FOURTEEN

OH! WHAT A LOVELY WAR!

'I am so cross,' said Mr Lovely as he marched back into his lovely living room, 'that I've got half a mind to write a VERY STRONGLY WORDED LETTER!'

'Yes, yes!' said Mrs Lovely, following him. She was actually **SHAKING WITH FURY**. 'Maybe we should even go one stage further than that,' she went on, 'and hand-deliver the letter wearing a QUITE ANGRY EXPRESSION.'

'I might even SAY SOMETHING as I deliver the letter,' said Mr Lovely, pacing up and down. 'I might use quite a RUDE WORD.'

Mrs Lovely gasped in shock. She knew she had just been very rude indeed to her sister Mrs Twit but she didn't expect Mr Lovely to follow suit.

'What sort of word?' she checked.

'I might say . . .

GOSH, YOU'RE A BAD APPLE,'

said Mr Lovely.

Mrs Lovely went pale and had to sit down. She had never before heard her lovely husband use such language. 'Anthony!' she said faintly. 'Control yourself!'

Here we see the problem with being TOO lovely. Mr and Mrs Lovely simply weren't able to work out what to do with their anger towards the Twits. Decades of loveliness had left them powerless when faced with such a pair of horrors. Mrs Lovely might have just declared war, but she was far, far too lovely to know how a war is waged. Luckily their children were there to help.

'**A BAD APPLE?**' said Ruff from the doorway.

'A strongly worded **LETTER?**' said Tumble.

'We've been telling you for weeks that those Twits have been playing tricks and trying to drive you away! Ruff, show them the notebook!'

Ruff pulled the evidence notebook from his pocket and showed it to Mr and Mrs Lovely. And this time, finally, they paid attention.

'See?' said Tumble. 'The bins, the tiger, the cakes . . . It was ALL the TWITS!'

'You're right,' said Mrs Lovely. 'First things first, we need to change THIS!' She pointed to the embroidered words hanging on the wall.

Ruff and Tumble looked at the Lovely Code.

Be lovely at all times to everybody
Give everybody a lovely day
Everybody is lovely underneath

'I think it's time the Lovely Code got a bit of an update,' announced Mrs Lovely.

'YES!' cheered Ruff. 'It's worked for a long time, but you never met any real Twits before!'

'We have been lovely for long enough!' decided Mrs Lovely, getting up from her chair. 'Mr Lovely, fetch me a pen!'

Mr Lovely handed Mrs Lovely a thick black marker and she went to work. A few seconds later, the Lovely Code looked like this:

Be lovely at all times to everybody
Except Twits

Give everybody a lovely day
Unless they are Twits

NOT *Everybody is lovely underneath*
Some people are just TWITS

'GO, MUM!' yelled the twins. 'That's more like it!'

'Do you know,' said Mr Lovely, examining the brand-new code, 'I think this sounds rather fun!'

'It will be enormous fun!' agreed Ruff. 'It'll be the best game EVER!'

'So how DO we start a war against those Twits?' asked Mrs Lovely. 'We've been lovely for so long, I'm not sure I know how.'

'We can help you there,' replied Tumble. 'The first thing we need is to work out what weapons we have.'

'I'm not sure we have any weapons,' she said. 'The only things we have are lovely! All my inventions are designed to give people a **LOVELY DAY** . . . and I'd like to give Mr and Mrs Twit the **WORST DAY!**'

'But, my darling,' said Mr Lovely suddenly, holding up a finger, 'don't you see? Those Twits HATE anything lovely!'

'She's right!' agreed Ruff. 'They can't stand colour or fun! I think you have all the weapons you need!'

Mrs Lovely thought for a long, long while. And

then she smiled a smile. It started off small but soon grew to the size of the actual moon.

'That looks like the face of somebody who just had an idea,' Ruff said to his sister.

'**IT IS!**' said Mrs Lovely, pulling them both into a hug. 'I've got a brilliant plan to get back at those Twits in the way they will HATE MOST IN THE WORLD.'

'What are we going to do?' asked Tumble excitedly.

'We are going to make them **NICE,**' started off Mrs Lovely. 'And then we are going to make them **POPULAR**. And then we are going to make them **USEFUL.**'

THERE WAS A
MOMENT OF SILENCE.

'Erm,' said Ruff, 'sorry . . . you want to make Mr and Mrs Twit NICE, POPULAR and USEFUL? Did I hear that right?'

'Yes, you did,' his mother replied. 'Listen.' And she told the rest of the Lovely family her incredibly clever and really rather unlovely idea.

'You're right – that IS brilliant!' said Mr Lovely when she had finished. 'It's the cleverest plan I've ever heard. We'll use our loveliness against them! We're going to cascade **KINDNESS** on those Twits!'

'We'll overpower them with **PLEASANTNESS**!' added Mrs Lovely.

'We'll heap their horrible hairy heads with **HELPFULNESS**!' shouted Ruff.

'We'll swamp them with **SWEETNESS**!' said Tumble.

172

'We'll bosh their big bottoms with **BENEVOLENCE!'** finished Mr Lovely, who was really getting into the swing of things.

'But to begin,' Mrs Lovely warned the twins, 'I need you to go somewhere completely terrifying.'

'We'll go ANYWHERE!' replied Tumble.

'Even to the worst place in the entire universe?' their mother asked.

'Yes, yes!' Ruff told her. 'What is this horrific, terrifying place?'

'MRS TWIT'S KNICKER DRAWER,' replied Mrs Lovely.

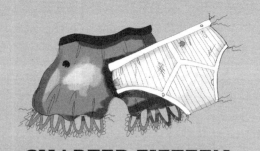

CHAPTER FIFTEEN

MRS TWIT'S
KNICKER DRAWER

A few days later, when a pitch-black night had fallen over the Twits' house, all was silent and still. No wind stirred the branches of the Big Dead Tree. No creature moved among the tall stinging nettles and thistles. Somewhere, far in the distance, a cow **BARKED**. Actually it might have been a dog – we're not sure. It probably was a dog, come to think of it. Anyway, something barked. But otherwise there was no sound at all.

If some animal with incredibly good eyesight had been there – perhaps an owl who had been living on carrots for the past year – it might have spotted movement in the large horse chestnut tree that spread its wide branches above the garden. But no carrot-eating owl was present. And so the Lovely twins went completely undetected as they began their difficult and dangerous mission.

THE WAR ON THE TWITS WAS ABOUT TO BEGIN.

As nimbly as freshly greased otters, the twins **SLID DOWN THE ROPE** into the Twits' garden. As quietly as a pair of mice wearing slippers, they crept through the thistles to the front door. Ever since Mr Twit had burst through it, with his bottom covered in wasps, it didn't shut properly. With a slight shove, it opened with a **LONG** and **SINISTER CREAK.**

Upstairs, Mr Twit turned over in his sleep. A strange

squeaky noise invaded the dream he was having, but it was a dream about a house made of halloumi cheese so it wasn't too out of place.

AS STEALTHILY AS A PAIR OF NINJA PANTHERS,

Ruff and Tumble crept through the Twits' house.

AS SOFTLY AS AN UNUSUALLY FLUFFY BABY PANDA,

they climbed the stairs.

AS SILENTLY AS A GIRAFFE WITH A SORE THROAT,

they tiptoed into the bedroom.

Without any windows, the Twits' bedroom was very dark indeed. But the twins had been here before and knew their way. Also, when you can't use your eyes, your other senses become even more powerful. The Lovely twins' ears – all four of them – could hear the **RATTLING**, **GASPING** snores coming from the beds at either side of the room. Their sensitive young feet could feel the direction of the floorboards so they could head in a straight line. And – there's no getting away from this and we hope you haven't just had your tea – their noses could pick up the smell from the chest of drawers where the Twits' clothes were kept.

What did it smell like? There are some things that cannot be described with words. And there are other things that, even though they COULD be described with words, are best left to the imagination. This chest of drawers was definitely one of those things.

AS SLOWLY AND CAREFULLY
AS A SNAIL MAKING ITS
WAY THROUGH A MINEFIELD,

the twins edged across the Twits' bedroom,
the snores on either side of them sounding like the

RATTLING OF TWO FILTHY
OLD TRAINS.

When they reached the chest of drawers, Ruff gently eased the topmost drawer open. He was half expecting something startling to happen, like a rat to jump out of it. But rats are actually rather intelligent animals. Certainly far too clever to hang about in Mrs Twit's knicker drawer.

In the faint moonlight that spilled up the stairs from the open door, Tumble could now see Mrs Twit's array of large bloomers laid out before her like folded parachutes. She slid the rucksack silently off her back and reached inside. She pulled out several pairs of purple-and-yellow pants and laid them carefully in the drawer. She nodded to Ruff:

MISSION ACCOMPLISHED.

It was at this point that the brave twins had to move on to an even more dangerous and disgusting part of their mission. We didn't tell you about it until now because we didn't want you to stop reading this book, give it a one-star review and then attempt to flush it down the toilet. For one thing you'd block your toilet. And for another thing, if you give us a one-star review, we'll come round to your house and cry.

Anyway — on to the most dangerous and disgusting part of the mission. You might think that Mrs Twit's knicker drawer is the most loathsome, inhospitable place on the planet.

But actually there is one place that is even **SCARIER.** Even **DANKER.** Even more **FOUL.**

AND IT IS THIS.
PREPARE YOURSELF.

MR TWIT'S
UNDERPANTS
DRAWER.

That's right. We're going there. Let's say it one more time for luck.

MR TWIT'S
UNDERPANTS
DRAWER.

NOW READ ON.

Ruff kneeled down and opened the very bottom drawer in the chest. It opened with a **SCRAPING**, **SCRATCHING** sound that made Mr Twit mutter in his sleep once more. He was now having a dream about a giant snake made of sandpaper so the noise also fitted in quite well. The twins waited, motionless, until he settled back down and began to snore again. Then Tumble reached once more into her backpack and laid several pairs of purple-and-yellow pants over the top of Mr Twit's own array of underwear. Fortunately it was far too dark to get a good look at them. Soundlessly Ruff closed the drawer and the twins retreated across the bedroom, throwing in a commando roll of triumph even though it wasn't strictly necessary.

The Lovely twins slipped **BACK
DOWN
THE STAIRS**
and out of the door. They flitted back through the garden like a pair of stealthy badgers who are also international superspies. Soon they were back in the tree house, nestling down to sleep with the tiger curled up at their feet. And when the Twits awoke in the morning, they had no idea that anything untoward had happened apart from the fact that a couple of Mr Twit's dreams had had unusually realistic sound effects.

CHAPTER SIXTEEN

THE INCREDIBLE DANCING TWITS

Mrs Twit woke up, got out of bed and got dressed. We don't need to hang about here and watch Mrs Twit getting dressed. Not because it feels impolite but because it would make us all feel badly sick for the next eighteen hours. The only detail you need is that Mrs Twit dressed in one of the pairs of pants that the twins had secreted in her drawer. She didn't notice that they were different to her normal bloomers because the windowless bedroom was so dark.

Once she was up and about, Mrs Twit went out into the garden to **STAMP** on some snails. Lots

THE INCREDIBLE DANCING TWITS

of gardeners don't like snails because they eat their lettuces or their flowers. Mrs Twit didn't care about any of that. She just liked stamping on things.

As well as stamping on the snails, Mrs Twit liked to give them names first. If you had been walking past her garden at that time of the morning you might have heard her horrible voice saying things like: 'Oh, hello, little snail. Your name is George. And guess what? TIME'S UP, GEORGE!' followed by a **SQUELCHING**, **STAMPY** NOISE.

'SAY YOUR PRAYERS, CLARENCE!' Mrs Twit screeched, cackling as she spotted a snail.

Just then her eye was caught by the yellow house with its brightly coloured curtains. Mrs Twit's good mood evaporated like a dirty puddle in the sun as she remembered that her sister was still living next door. For a split second a dark cloud of worry scudded across her mind as she recalled Mrs Lovely shouting, 'THIS MEANS WAR!' But then she shook herself and snorted. What could such a kindly person possibly do?

SHE WAS ABOUT TO FIND OUT.

In the meantime Mr Twit also got out of bed. He also got dressed, and once again let's not linger on that particular event. All you need to know is that beneath his stained old trousers, he put on his own pair of the purple-and-yellow underpants that had been hidden in his drawer in the dark bedroom. Then he stomped downstairs and joined Mrs Twit in the garden.

Mr Twit was intending to suggest to Mrs Twit that they should try to borrow a wrecking ball and knock the Lovelies' house down while they were still in it. But he never got that far. Because all of a sudden something incredibly strange started to happen.

As she prepared to stamp on Clarence the snail, one of Mrs Twit's legs unexpectedly stuck out sideways at an odd angle and both her arms shot into the air. Her bottom began to rotate in an odd and decidedly untwittish fashion.

'What on earth do you think you're doing, you

squidgy banana?' said Mr Twit, taking a step back and looking at her in confusion.

'I'm not quite sure,' said Mrs Twit, lowering her arms and using her hands to stop her hips moving. 'Something very strange just came over me and I felt like I needed to –'

At this point, both her legs began to kick as she hopped about on the spot. Her legs carried her down the garden path and out into the street, high-kicking furiously with her hands on her hips.

'Come back! What are you doing?' yelled Mr Twit, chasing after her. 'People will **LOOK AT YOU!** Stop it!'

'I CAN'T stop it!' wailed Mrs Twit. By now she had reached the corner of the street and was heading into town, with her old boots tapping out a rhythm on the road as she high-kicked along.

'It almost looks like you're . . . I can hardly bring myself to say the word.' Mr Twit was so aghast that he failed to realize that he too had started **JIGGING** about. 'It looks like you're **DANCING!**'

'Well, you're dancing too!' pointed out Mrs Twit, gesturing at his legs.

Mr Twit looked down and let out an enormous scream.

'YEEEAAAARGH!'

You won't be surprised to hear that neither Twit liked dancing. They regarded it as an enormous waste of time – and it seemed to make people far too cheerful. But dancing is exactly what they had both started to do. And this is why.

Remember when the Lovely Bus held a little dance party earlier on in the story and Mrs Lovely used one of her brilliant inventions, **DISCO PANTS?** Well, as you might have worked out for yourself, Ruff and Tumble had put several pairs of these Disco Pants in Mr and Mrs Twit's underwear drawers. Not only that but these were special **EXTRA-STRONG** versions. The normal pants just make you want to have a little bop, which is something that can cheer up anybody's day. But these new supercharged Disco Pants, on the other hand, were so strong that they forced you to dance **WILDLY** and **UNCONTROLLABLY.** And the effects were only just starting.

The town centre was busy with people getting ready for the Springtime Parade, which was due to take place the very next day. Everybody was working hard, cleaning, decorating and laying out long tables ready for a big outdoor feast the whole town would share. Imagine their surprise when a pair of dirty Twits danced their way into the main square, their feet tapping frantically on the cobbles and their legs kicking out like a couple of jolly giraffes.

The people in the square began to form a circle round Mr and Mrs Twit as they jigged about. The crowd started clapping and cheering. At that moment the Lovely Bus pulled up. Mrs Lovely, grinning, flicked a switch and loud music filled the air. The cheers and applause grew louder as the Twits danced around wildly.

'What . . . are . . . we . . . doing?' asked Mrs Twit, pogoing up and down on the spot and doing air guitar.

'I . . . don't . . . know . . .' growled Mr Twit angrily, dropping to his front and doing the worm.

The people around them had started dancing too. A group of workers in hard hats were operating a crane nearby, removing a statue from its plinth. (The statue was being taken away for cleaning, leaving the plinth empty. This might seem like an irrelevant detail but it isn't.) The workers started jumping and jiggling as well, clapping and cheering the incredible dancing Twits.

'I . . .
HATE . . .
DANCING . . .' snarled Mrs Twit, leaping into the air and doing a pirouette before landing delicately on her toes. 'Oooh, me bunions!'

'I . . .
HATE . . .
DANCING . . .
TOO,' replied Mr Twit, bending at the waist and doing an impression of a dancing robot.

By now the crowd was going absolutely wild. People ran to fetch their friends or telephoned their families to come and see these amazing dancing people. Many people had seen the Twits out and about before – but never dancing. Normally they were just muttering to themselves or, in the case of Mrs Twit, trying to attack animals with her stick.

The Twits were wearing such powerful Disco Pants that they danced in front of the townsfolk for four whole hours. By the time the pants started to wear out, their shoes were actually smoking from the forty minutes of high-energy coordinated tap-dancing they had just completed. A news crew from

the local TV station had arrived some time ago and been filming their performance for the main bulletin that evening. Mrs Twit had shouted some very rude things at them, but the music was far too loud for anyone to hear.

At last the pants' power was spent and the Twits realized that they were in control of their own arms and legs again. As soon as this happened, they broke through the excited ring of people surrounding them and scurried off towards their house as fast as their exhausted feet would take them.

'BRAVO!'

shouted the townsfolk.

'AMAZING!

ENCORE!

DO SOME MORE DANCING!

YOU'RE THE BEST!'

'You cheered me right up!' said a man in a round purple hat to Mr Twit as he passed, slapping him on the back. 'I don't even care that my house is yellow any more!'

'You're an inspiration!' shouted a lady to Mrs Twit. 'I'm going to sign up for dance lessons first thing tomorrow! You're my hero!'

'We seem to have made these people HAPPY,' spat Mr Twit in disgust.

At this point an angelic-looking young girl named Amelie appeared beside him.

'I just wanted to say thank you,' said the angelic little girl named Amelie. 'It's wonderful the way you and your wife dance together. I wish you were my grandad! You must be the most fun grandad in the whole world.'

It was a speech that could have melted the stoniest of stony hearts. Well, it could have done unless the heart in question belonged to an enormous great twit. **'GED OUTTAVIT!'** said Mr Twit, shoving the angelic little girl backwards into a puddle. And, stopping their ears so they couldn't hear the shouts and cries of their fans, the newly famous Twits left the square and vanished into the back streets of the town.

Mr and Mrs Lovely watched them leave, before

getting out of the bus and walking over to the TV news crew.

'I say,' said Mrs Lovely to the reporter, 'would you like to know where those lovely dancing people live? Because they happen to be our next-door neighbours.'

'Amazing!' said the reporter. 'We'd love to interview them and find out what makes them dance so wonderfully.'

Mrs Lovely grinned from ear to ear. 'Follow us.'

CHAPTER SEVENTEEN

COMPLIMENTARY BEER

Mr and Mrs Twit flung themselves through their front door and slammed it firmly behind them. They were both absolutely exhausted from their hours of dancing, but more than that they were appalled at the reception they had been given.

'They LIKED us,' said Mrs Twit shakily, lowering herself into a comfortable chair with a click of her rickety hips. 'They actually LIKED US.'

'Stop it,' said Mr Twit, wiping his brow. 'You're making me feel all **TWIRLY.**'

He moved to the cabinet and poured himself an

extra-large mug of calming beer from one of the bottles arranged there.

'Give us one!' begged Mrs Twit. 'I'm absolutely parched.'

Mr Twit would normally have refused – or played some mean trick like half-filling the beer with salt – but he was too shaken up to bother. He poured some into a second mug and handed it to Mrs Twit. They both sat in their chairs drinking, giving an occasional shiver as they remembered what had just happened.

'They were all **LOOKING AT US,'** said Mrs Twit, taking a large gulp of beer.

'LOOKING AT US!' agreed Mr Twit, shuddering. It had been, without a doubt, the single worst day of his entire life. Worse, even, than the day he'd fallen into the hedge and his beard had been accidentally combed as he scrambled his way out.

'It must have been that rotten SISTER,' said Mrs Twit darkly as she bent over her beer mug.

'But how?' asked Mr Twit, getting up to fetch more beer and topping up their drinks.

'She's played some kind of TRICK on us,' replied Mrs Twit, taking another huge mouthful.

'But WE play the tricks!' said Mr Twit, choking slightly. 'THIS IS **MONSTROUS!**'

'Is there any more beer?' asked Mrs Twit after a while, as she drained her mug for the seventh time.

Mr Twit got up once again to fetch another bottle.

'It's nicer than usual,' he said, topping up his own mug. 'Did you buy a different sort?'

'No,' said Mrs Twit, holding out her mug. 'It's the same old brown beer we always get. But you're right – it does taste better today. Perhaps they're using a new recipe.'

If either of the Twits had really stopped to think, they might have realized at this point that something strange was going on. They might even have started to wonder whether somebody could have been tampering with the bottles of beer in the cabinet. If they had really thought about it, they might have worked out that somebody had sneaked into their house and poured something into the beer before carefully resealing the bottles. But they didn't work any of this out because they were too **BRAIN-BATTERED** from all the dancing.

'Woss that noise?' said Mr Twit presently, as he finished his eleventh mug of nicer-than-usual beer.

Mrs Twit cupped a hand behind her ear. Sure enough, a strange sound was coming from outside their house. It was the low hum of conversation — like the noise of a theatre audience before the show begins.

'It sounds like there's PEOPLE out there,' said Mrs Twit angrily. 'Horrible chattering PEOPLE. Go and tell them to hop it, Mr Twit.'

'I shall,' said Mr Twit, getting up from his chair with a slight sloshing noise. His tummy was very, very full of fizzy beer. With one hand on his straining belly, he marched to the door and poked his head outside.

'THERE HE IS!' said a voice.

And all at once a great cheer went up. Flashbulbs went off in Mr Twit's face as he stood on the doorstep, staring. Mrs Twit levered herself out of her chair, also feeling extremely full of beer, and joined him on the doorstep. There, gathered at their front-garden fence, was the TV news crew alongside several photographers and a large crowd of people who had come to see where the wonderful dancing couple lived.

'And there's his wife too!' said the TV reporter excitedly into his microphone. 'We've tracked the lovely dancing couple down to their home! Aren't they just the most charming pair you ever saw?'

Mr Twit, with Mrs Twit trailing along behind him, stomped up towards the front gate. He was fully prepared to give everyone a talking-to that they wouldn't forget.

'We're not a lovely dancing couple,' he was planning to say. 'We hate lovely things, ESPECIALLY dancing. And we hate ALL OF YOU! So why don't you just GET OUT OF HERE and leave us alone before I start hitting you all with the garden rake?'

That's what Mr Twit was PLANNING to say. But when he opened his mouth that isn't what happened. Instead Mr Twit let out an

ENORMOUS BURP.

The **BIGGEST,**
LOUDEST,
L O N G E S T
BURP

you ever heard in your life. And along with the burp came some very unexpected words.

'HOW NICE TO SEE YOU ALL,' burped Mr Twit into the reporter's face. 'WELCOME TO OUR HOME.'

Mrs Twit was astonished to hear these words come out of her husband's mouth. Even in the form of a huge burp, they were the nicest things she had ever heard him say. *The silly turnip must be going soft in the head,* she thought to herself – and she opened her mouth to say, 'IGNORE HIM. GET OUT OF HERE BEFORE I GET MY STICK OUT AND START THWACKING!'

She opened her mouth to say this, but when she did so, something else unexpected happened. Mrs Twit let out her own

BURP

‑ just as **LOUD**

and **LONG.**

And along with this burp came the following words: **'WOULD ANYONE LIKE A NICE CUP OF TEA?'**

Mrs Twit clamped her hands over her mouth in horror.

What on earth was going on? You've probably worked it out for yourself by now. Remember Mrs Lovely's invention Nice Pop? The special drinks that make you burp out something lovely every time you take a sip? Well, Mrs Lovely had brewed up a special extra‑strong batch and used it to alter the Twits' beer.

It had actually been Ruff and Tumble's idea – and it was working brilliantly.

'I LIKE YOUR HAIR,' burped Mr Twit to a nearby photographer.

'YOU LOOK LOVELY TODAY,' belched Mrs Twit as soon as she took her hands away from her mouth.

A lady who was leaning over the fence giggled and went red. 'Thank you,' she replied.

To the Twits' complete horror, the complimentary burps kept on coming. Their stomachs were so swollen with fizzy beer mixed with Nice Pop that they just couldn't help themselves. Mrs Lovely had brewed up such a strong batch of her marvellous formula that they even started being nice to each other.

'YOU LOOK VERY HANDSOME,' burped Mrs Twit to Mr Twit.

He looked at her in complete disbelief and opened his mouth to say, 'Shut up, you silly bag!' but instead found himself belching out:

'I LOVE YOU'

at high volume (which is not easy to do).

The crowd at the front gate went, **'AAAHHHHH!'**

'Romance is not dead!' said the reporter. 'This saintly couple still love each other after so long together. Isn't that inspiring? Mr Twit –' he held out his microphone – 'could you tell our viewers your secret? How do you keep the magic alive in your marriage?'

'SHE'S LOVELY!' burped Mr Twit.

'AND HE'S A RIGHT DISH!' added Mrs Twit among the biggest belch yet.

There was another **'AAAHHH'** from the crowd.

'Well, there you have it,' said the reporter into the camera. 'These charming old people still find each other beautiful. And isn't there a lesson there for all of us?'

Mr and Mrs Twit were both desperate to say something incredibly rude, but neither of them dared open their mouths for fear of the horrific things that might come out. They scampered back into their house and went straight to bed, even though it was only the middle of the afternoon.

CHAPTER EIGHTEEN

THE WORLD'S MOST FAMOUS TWITS

Now we begin to see the sheer genius of Mrs Lovely's plan. She had promised to make the Twits **NICE**, **POPULAR** and **USEFUL**. She had already made them nice using the Disco Pants and the Complimentary Beer. Now for the final and most brilliant stage of her plan. And she was going to put this final stage into action in front of the whole town. She planned to make the Twits USEFUL in a way that would fix them once and for all.

The following morning, the newspaper plopped through the Lovely letterbox and Mrs Lovely looked at it with great satisfaction.

'Our plan is working!' she told the twins. 'Quickly, rush next door and put this newspaper under the Twits' door. I want them to see what's going on!'

Ruff and Tumble climbed up to the tree house, raced along the branch and

SLID
DOWN
THE
ROPE into the Twits'

garden. They could just have run round through the front gate, but that's not nearly so much fun. Tumble had the newspaper clutched in her teeth and they slipped it beneath the front door before climbing back up the rope and away.

Mr Twit had just stomped downstairs when he saw the newspaper appear on the doormat. He hadn't ordered a paper, but he grabbed it anyway to see what the headline was. He was hoping it would be something horrible that he could cut out and stick into the **DAILY TWIT.** A children's hospital being invaded by bees, perhaps. Or a rare giant panda stubbing its toe. But when he picked up the paper and looked at the front page, his jaw almost hit the floor in horror.

There, right on the front of the newspaper, was a photograph of Mr and Mrs Twit inside a large heart. The headline above this read:

TWIT MUST BE LOVE!
CHARMING COUPLE INSPIRE TOWN

Choking and gasping, Mr Twit squinted at the article beneath the photograph.

Despite their unusual name, Mr and Mrs Twit have become overnight celebrities. This generous pair spent the whole afternoon putting on a dance show to cheer up the town. And, boy, can these lovely folks move! They treated the crowds to several hours of dance, taking in a tap dance as well as some incredible breakdancing, which featured Mr Twit spinning on his head!

Mr Twit reached up and rubbed the top of his head before reading on.

We tracked these dancers down to their house, where we were treated to a charming sight as Mr Twit was seen by the whole town telling his wife that he still loves her even after so many years together. It's enough to melt your heart! The couple were so overcome with emotion that they had to head back inside. But the grateful townsfolk have been busily thinking of a way to celebrate these inspiring Twits. And rumour has it that they'll become a main feature at today's Springtime Parade!

Mr Twit could read no more. He bundled up the newspaper up and threw it into the fireplace where it landed with a **WHUMPH,** sending up a cloud of soot.

Mrs Twit, hearing this, shouted down the stairs to find out what was happening.

'What's going on, you daft wombat?' is what Mrs Twit had intended to say. But unfortunately the Complimentary Beer had not yet worn off. So what she, in fact, said – or burped, rather – was this: **'GOOD MORNING, MY SWEET LOVE!'**

Mr Twit opened his mouth to reply, 'What are you going on about, you scruffy mongoose?' But instead he found himself belching, **'DID YOU SLEEP WELL, MY LOVELY DARLING?'**

Upstairs, Mrs Twit decided to turn on the radio rather than attempt to say anything else. She was already bright red from sheer fury. But the radio didn't distract her. Instead she tuned in right in the middle of a news report . . .

'These LOVELY people,' the reporter was saying, 'as well as being great dancers, are still very much in love after decades together. Have a listen to this . . .'

And then Mrs Twit went redder still as she heard her own voice coming out of the radio.

'HE'S A RIGHT DISH!' she was saying.

'Oooh, let's hear that again!' said the radio presenter.
'I love these guys.'

'HE'S A RIGHT DISH!'

'Again!'

'HE'S A RIGHT DISH!'

Mrs Twit grabbed the radio and tried to throw
it out of the window. As we know, the Twits' house
doesn't have any windows, so instead she just threw
it against the wall. It broke into pieces and fell to
the floor – but before it died completely she was still
treated to the sound of her own voice saying, **'HE'S
A RIGHT DISH!'** three or four more times.

Mr Twit thundered up the stairs, holding a notepad and a pencil. Not trusting himself to speak, he had decided to write everything down.

WHAT'S GOING ON, YOU WRINKLY OLD WITCH?

he scribbled in his large untidy handwriting.

Mrs Twit grabbed the notebook and wrote her reply.

How should I know, you UGLY, HAIRY baboon?

OUR REPUTATION IS IN TATTERS!
wrote Mr Twit. *PEOPLE THINK WE ARE NICE! WE HAVE BECOME POPULAR!*

For most people, everyone thinking you're a lovely person would actually be a great reputation to have. But not for the Twits, of course. They wanted people to think they were FOUL so they would be left well alone.

We'd better do something horrible quickly, wrote Mrs Twit. You bristly BOG BRUSH.

She was unable to resist writing an insult at the end through sheer force of habit.

Both Twits stampeded down the stairs, intending to go out into the town and do as many foul things as possible. But when they came out of their front door, they both stopped in their tracks.

Something completely unbelievable was happening on the street in front of their house.

CHAPTER NINETEEN
THE GRAND TWIT PARADE

The street in front of the Twits' house was entirely filled with people. And every single one was staring right at them. The eyes of Mr and Mrs Twit boggled and spun like small Catherine wheels at this horrific sight. It was their **WORST NIGHTMARE** come true.

'Good morning, Mr and Mrs Twit!' shouted Mrs Lovely, who was standing at their garden gate wearing a smile the size of a spacehopper. 'Look! Everybody thinks that you are so **LOVELY** that the Springtime Parade has made a special detour to give you pride of place! Come on, everybody! Let's begin the celebration!'

'**HOORAY!**' shouted the crowd, as the Twits stood on their doorstep with their mouths opening and closing like landed fish. One person was even carrying a placard that read:

WE LOVE THE DANCING TWITS!

in large red and yellow letters.

The cheering people surged through the front gate like a tide and swept up Mr and Mrs Twit, lifting them up high and carrying them towards a float at the head of the parade. As they passed through the gate, a brass band started to play a stirring march.

A HUGE BURP

came from Mrs Twit as she was lifted on to the float and plonked into a golden chair. '**THIS IS WONDERFUL!**'

'**WHAT A NICE SURPRISE,**' said Mr Twit through a gigantic belch – the Complimentary Beer had still not worn off.

The cheers grew louder still.

'Our plan is going perfectly,' Mrs Lovely told her family as the Springtime Parade moved off. 'We've made the Twits famous! Everyone thinks they're LOVELY!'

'And until the Nice Pop wears off, there's absolutely nothing they can do about it!' added Tumble.

'Brilliant plan, Mum!' added Ruff.

'That was just Phase One!' Mrs Lovely reminded him. 'Now it's time to show the whole town that NOT everybody is lovely underneath . . .'

'Some people are JUST TWITS!' said Mr Lovely, cycling up in the Lovely Bus. 'Come on, Lovely family! Hop on board! Let's fix those horrible Twits once and for all!'

Mrs Lovely and the twins leaped into the bus and the Tame Tiger joined them with a

ROAR.

Mr Lovely began to pedal and the bus followed the parade as it snaked its way towards the town square. Everyone had turned out to make a fuss of their new celebrities. The mayor was there, looking splendid in her red robes and thick gold chains. Even Herbert Slobgollion the Tiger Tamer was in attendance — you could see his tall black hat bobbing along in the middle of the crowd.

And you're never in a million years going to believe what happened next.

Mr and Mrs Twit were driven in splendour through the streets. All along the route, smiling people cheered and shouted their names. It really was the loveliest thing you ever saw on a bright sunny day. The band played, the crowds applauded. And, gradually, something began to happen to the Twits' faces. Mrs Twit's scowl became slightly less downward-facing. Mr Twit's beard jutted out in a less angry way. The wrinkles on their frowny foreheads seemed to smooth out. And, all at once, Mr Twit let out a

GREAT
BIG LAUGH.

Beside him, Mrs Twit broke into a gigantic smile for the first time in ages. And as they smiled and laughed, the years seemed to fall from them until there, sitting at the head of the parade, were two much younger people with good thoughts shining out of their faces like sunbeams.

The Twits had finally learned how wonderful it is to be kind and happy. And from that day forth they became the two smiliest, most apple-cheeked pair of old lovelies the town had ever seen. They started a business looking after abandoned puppies and everybody lived happily ever after and loved each other and there was no pain or suffering in the whole world ever again.

THE END

HA HA, only joking. You didn't fall for that, did you? What kind of a silly story do you think this is?

Here's what actually happened. It's far more **HORRIBLE** but a lot more **FUN.**

Mr and Mrs Twit were driven in splendour through the streets. All along the route, smiling people cheered and shouted their names. It really was the loveliest thing you ever saw on a bright sunny day. The band played, the crowds applauded. And at last the Springtime Parade rolled into the main square.

Here, a huge feast had been laid on for the whole town. There were long tables absolutely groaning with cream cakes and sandwiches and sausage rolls. There were bowls filled with chocolate bars of every kind, and jars of sweets for anybody to help themselves to. There were golden chicken drumsticks and fresh bread rolls with butter. There were platters of cheese and sliced roasted meats. And at the head of the biggest table were two thrones for the guests of honour. Mr and Mrs Twit were lowered from their float with ceremony and ushered to their places,

ready for the feast to begin. They tried to complain, but every time they opened their mouths they just burped out something nice.

'Welcome to the Springtime Parade!' said the mayor, grabbing a microphone. The crowd cheered. 'And before we tuck into the feast,' she went on, 'I think we should hear a word from the town's LOVELIEST residents! They dance, they are kind to each other, they are an inspiration to us all! Please raise your glasses and toast . . .**THE TWITS!'**

'THE TWITS!' echoed the whole town, lifting their drinks into the air.

At this point, the mayor made a move that, in hindsight, turned out to be a mistake. She handed the microphone to Mrs Twit. Now, she didn't realize it was a mistake, of course. She had only heard Mrs Twit say – or rather burp – lovely kind things, because she had been under the influence of the beer mixed with Nice Pop. But what the mayor didn't realize is that during the parade the effects of Mrs Lovely's incredible potion had finally worn off.

Mrs Twit cleared her throat with a horrible noise like sharpened bats being scraped down a blackboard. She was slightly nervous to say anything in case another nice-sounding burp came out of her mouth, but it didn't. For the first time in a whole day she found that she was able to speak normally.

The townsfolk edged forward, eager to hear what inspiring thing this lovely lady might say next. Mrs Twit looked out across the expectant crowd and brought the microphone close to her twisted mouth with a piercing squeak of feedback.

'You lot,' said Mrs Twit, her amplified voice echoing from the tall buildings that surrounded the square, 'are the biggest load of

SILLY,
UGLY,
USELESS NINCOMPOOPS
I'VE EVER SEEN.'

There were a few nervous laughs, but otherwise the packed square was totally silent.

'Why don't you bunch of cheering, grinning dishcloths just leave us alone?' went Mrs Twit's amplified voice through the speakers. 'We **HATE** you, and we **HATE** this town, and we **HATE** your ridiculous parade and we **HATE** this disgusting-looking feast.

HATE,
HATE,
HATE!
GRAAAGGGHHH!'

Beside her, Mr Twit nodded in foul agreement and made a rude gesture at the mayor.

Nobody made any noise at all for a few seconds, apart from the trombone player in the brass band who accidentally produced a small **PARP** from his instrument. The whole town was stunned into a shocked silence by this mean outburst.

But then somebody spoke.

Ruff and Tumble had worked their way to the front of the crowd. It was time to put the very last part of their plan into action.

'Well, you,' said Tumble, 'are a pair of ungrateful, **NASTY TWITS!'**

'Yeah!' added Ruff. 'These nice people made you special guests at the town parade. And if you're too twisted and mean and horrible to even say thank you, well . . .'

And Ruff picked up the largest cream cake he could see and shoved it straight into Mrs Twit's shocked face.

And that's when things really started to kick off.

CHAPTER TWENTY

THE GREAT FOOD FIGHT

For a long moment Mrs Twit just stood there with cream slowly dripping off her chin and a slice of strawberry stuck to her nose.

Mr Twit glared at the twins. 'Why, you little –'

Tumble interrupted him. 'Oh, SHUT UP, you barmy bristle-bearded old dustbin!'

She grabbed another large cream cake and shoved this squarely into Mr Twit's face. It stuck fast to his beard with a **SPLAT.**

'RIGHT!' bellowed Mrs Twit, who had finally regained the power of speech. She lurched forward, picked Tumble up by the ankles, held her upside down and dunked her head into a gigantic bowl of custard that had been placed in the middle of the feast.

And that is how the Great Food Fight began.

Mrs Lovely, who was nearby and fully prepared for battle, uttered a **GREAT SHOUT** of **RAGE** and began to fling chicken wings at Mrs Twit's head. Some of these bounced off and hit members of the crowd, who reached for other items of food to defend themselves. Within seconds the entire town square was a maelstrom of flying food. Much of it was aimed at Mr and Mrs Twit, who were soon covered with cream, grease and dips as the townsfolk punished them for spoiling the party. But once a food fight gets properly started the rules tend to go out of the window. It's the same with any fight, to be fair.

Even the mayor ended up joining in after she was

hit in the eye by a Cornish pasty. She abandoned her black hat and plunged her hands into a trifle, flinging gobbets of jelly and spongy biscuits at Mr Twit, who was defending himself as best he could with a silver tray. Mrs Twit crouched beside him. She had taken off one of her holey old stockings and was using it as a slingshot, sending mini sausage rolls into the crowd with deadly accuracy. Several people were knocked over as savoury snacks went **PA-DOINGING** into their faces at high velocity.

The Lovely twins were having the time of their lives. Tumble had scraped herself mainly clean of custard and they leaped on to the back of their friend the Tame Tiger, who went galloping around the battle like cavalry in a war of olden times. Ruff had grabbed a baguette and aimed it like a knight with a lance as the tiger went racing towards Mr Twit with his tray shield, roaring like anything. With precise aim, Ruff knocked the tray from his hands and the undefended Mr Twit was immediately spattered with chunks of trifle thrown by the mayor.

At this point the tiger, **SNARLING** with triumph, spotted Herbert Slobgollion covered from head to toe in meat-pie filling. It gave a blood-curdling

ROAR.

and sprang at him. Slobgollion turned tail in panic and fled home as fast as his legs would carry him. We're sorry (but not that sorry) to say that when he got there the other tigers immediately gobbled him up. This happened for two reasons:

1) he had spent many years being cruel to them and they had finally run out of patience, and 2) he was covered with beef and gravy, which was delicious. Anyway, we don't have to concern ourselves with him any more. His story is over – but the story of Mr and Mrs Twit has not quite reached its horrific conclusion, so let's return to the food fight in the town square.

By now the Twits were entirely surrounded by angry townsfolk. These people had gone to a great deal of trouble to put on today's parade – some of them had been up all night baking pies or sewing bunting – and now the whole thing had been ruined by the Twits, who instead of being a pair of lovely dancers had revealed themselves to be a mean pair of complete horribles. The townspeople, quite understandably, felt cheated. They advanced on Mr and Mrs Twit armed with various party snacks, **GROWLING** and **MUTTERING** angrily.

It was at this moment that Mr and Mrs Lovely put the final part of their plan into operation. Mrs Lovely pushed her way to the front of the crowd, wearing the backpack and nozzle that she usually used to paint houses.

'Oh, not again!' said a man in a purple hat standing nearby.

'YOU,' said Mrs Lovely, 'ARE THE MOST RUDE, UNKIND PAIR OF TWITS IN THE WHOLE WORLD!'

'WE KNOW!' shouted back Mrs Twit. 'And we'd have been quite happy if you'd just **LEFT US ALONE!'**

'YEAH!' yelled Mr Twit.

'Don't you even care that I'm your **TWIN SISTER?'** asked Mrs Lovely, who couldn't help giving Mrs Twit one last chance.

'NO, I DON'T!' screeched Mrs Twit, lifting a Scotch egg in preparation for combat. **'I DON'T LIKE SISTERS AND I DON'T LIKE YOU!'**

'In that case,' said Mrs Lovely, 'it is time for the final punishment. I made you **NICE**. I made you **POPULAR**. And now . . . for the first time in your whole twittish lives . . . you are going to be **USEFUL!**'

'NEVER!' screamed Mrs Twit, who hated the idea of being useful. It was against everything she believed.

Mrs Lovely stood up straight and tall and met her twin sister's gaze.

'ATTACK!'

she roared like a commander leading her troops into battle.

And the townspeople followed her as if she was some kind of cream-cake-wielding general. Together, they forced the Twits backwards, pelting them with food. Ruff and Tumble were at the front, flinging cupcakes for all they were worth and uttering blood-curdling war cries. Tumble had painted stripes of jam on her cheeks to make herself look especially fearsome.

There was an empty plinth in the centre of the town square. Usually it supported a large statue, but this had been taken away for cleaning during a brief passage that you may have completely missed in Chapter Sixteen. Anyway, the plinth had so much food piled up beside it that the Twits, as they were forced backwards by the crowd, soon ended up right on top of it. The food had formed a convenient ramp – which had all been part of Mrs Lovely's clever plan.

'It's time to teach you a **LESSON YOU WILL NEVER FORGET!'** said Mrs Lovely. 'You don't like people looking at you? Well . . . **YOU'D BETTER GET USED TO IT!** It's time for the Twits to be

USEFUL!' And Mrs Lovely activated

her paint sprayer.

Now, as you might remember, Mrs Lovely normally used this clever device to repaint houses or other things in bright, cheerful colours. But today she had loaded her backpack with a very special new kind of paint she had invented. It was silvery-grey in colour and was mixed with a special super-strong glue called **GNARLY GRIP**. And so when she turned it on the Twits were sprayed from head to foot within a second. And, within another three seconds, the glue-filled paint had set fast. And instead of Mr and Mrs Twit on the plinth in the town square, there stood two brand-new statues.

'Tumble!' called Mrs Lovely. 'You're up!'

Tumble walked to the foot of the plinth, wearing her own backpack and holding a paint sprayer. She pulled the trigger and on the side of the plinth that wasn't covered in food she sprayed in enormous letters the words

DON'T BE A TWIT.

'There,' said Mrs Lovely, looking at the new centrepiece to the town square in satisfaction. 'A little reminder for everybody. How very useful.'

CHAPTER TWENTY-ONE

THE STATUES IN
THE SQUARE

By sticking out their tongues, Mr and Mrs Twit were able to make small air holes at the corners of their mouths. By blinking frantically, they were able to clear the paint from their eyes. But otherwise they were completely coated in hard GNARLY GRIP glue. They could not move a muscle. Not even the small muscles in their toes.

'**THERE!**' declared Mrs Lovely. 'Now you two are finally **USEFUL.**'

And, dusting her hands together, she marched back to the Lovely Bus, with Mr Lovely and the twins following in her wake, feeling extremely proud and ever so slightly scared of her. She was no longer quite so lovely, but there was no denying that she was really very impressive. And perhaps after all, in this strange world, it's hard to be lovely all the time – especially with so many complete twits about.

The people of the town began to clear away the remnants of the Great Food Fight and by that evening the town square looked just as it had before – with one crucial difference. On a plinth in the centre were statues of two mean-looking people, one of them holding a wooden stick in one hand and a Scotch egg in the other. And beneath them, for all to see, was sprayed the warning:

DON'T BE A TWIT.

After all, it's pretty good advice.

And there Mr and Mrs Twit stayed as statues. After a few days, people got used to seeing them up there and many walked by without even looking up. Others stopped to stare at the horrible-looking statues and ponder on the message.

Mr and Mrs Lovely decided, after a lot of thought, to move to another town. They concluded that they had brought as much loveliness to this particular place as possible. It was time to spread happiness somewhere else. But they kept the Lovely Code as it was:

Be lovely at all times to everybody
Except Twits

Give everybody a lovely day
Unless they are Twits

NOT *Everybody is lovely underneath*
Some people are just TWITS

Because, after all, you never know when you're going to run into a twit, do you?

★

After the removal van had taken away their furniture and the workshop had been packed up, Mr Lovely jumped into the driving seat of the Lovely Bus and prepared to pedal.

Mrs Lovely, with a sigh, took one last look over at the Twits' house: windowless, dirty and deserted.

'It would have been nice to have a sister,' she said to herself sadly. 'But not a sister like that.' And with a sniff she followed the twins on to the bus.

Then Mr Lovely began pedalling, and with a final **TING** the Lovely Bus left the house forever.

As they neared the town centre, there was a growl and the Tame Tiger appeared from a side street. The twins laughed with delight as it leaped into the back to join them on their next adventure.

Mr Lovely cycled the Lovely Bus through the town square. There, high on their plinth, were the statues that were Mr and Mrs Twit. And, as usual, a small crowd had gathered, looking up at them.

'BYE, TWITS!' yelled Ruff and Tumble, waving.

'I wish you had been a bit more lovely,' said Mrs

Lovely, waving a handkerchief out of the window of the Lovely Bus. 'But, as I've recently discovered . . . not everybody is lovely underneath. **SOME PEOPLE ARE JUST TWITS.'**

The Lovely Bus trundled away and was never seen in that town again.

Up on the plinth, Mrs Twit watched it go. She had a pigeon sitting on her and at that exact moment the pigeon did a large and extravagant toilet all over her head.

'BRRRRRHHHHHH,'

said Mrs Twit through the small air hole at the corner of her mouth.

'What is it now, you ossified aardvark?' said Mr Twit through his own air hole.

'This filthy feathery frump just did its dirty business all over me!' complained the statue of Mrs Twit. The bird's droppings dripped into her eye.

Mr Twit laughed until the pigeon fluttered over to his own head and did exactly the same thing.

'GRRRRPH,' he huffed. 'If I ever get out of here, I will take a horrible revenge on ALL BIRDS! I'll catch them and . . . and make 'em into a PIE. Every single week!'

The people below were laughing and pointing

upwards as the bird droppings dripped down Mr Twit's stone beard.

'They're **LOOKING AT US** again!' said Mrs Twit furiously. 'Can't you stop them?'

'How am I supposed to do that, you mangy moorhen?' said Mr Twit. 'I'm a **STATUE, ENT I?'**

And that was the genius of Mrs Lovely's revenge. Because there Mr and Mrs Twit were forced to stay, with the whole town passing by and staring at them. They could do absolutely nothing about it. It was their worst nightmare come true.

And that, as they say in this business, is the end of the story.

Did the Twits ever manage to escape from their plinth?

Did they ever stop being statues and live to twit another day?

Did Mr Twit take his horrible revenge on all birds by baking them into a pie?

WELL . . .

THAT'S
ANOTHER STORY.

ORDINARY KIDS.
EXTRAORDINARY ADVENTURES.
LAUGHS FOR THE WHOLE FAMILY.

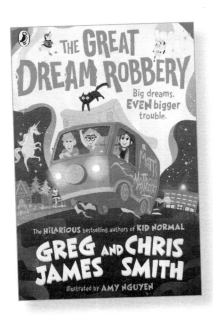

From the incredible imagination of
CHRIS SMITH...